THE GHOST OF LOVE

Diana had thought never to see Mr. Gerald Carshin again after he had vanished from her life without a word of warning.

But now he had reappeared out of the blue, to claim her as if the eight years of their separation never had existed.

She heard his passionate words of endearment breathed into her ear. She felt his strong arms around her, holding her fast. Then his lips with practiced skill came down on hers.

This was the moment Diana had dreaded for so long without daring to admit it even to herself. For this was the test of her strength and resolve, which she desperately feared she would fail just as she had before. . . .

THE
REPENTANT
REBEL

SIGNET Regency Romances You'll Want to Read

THE
REPENTANT
REBEL

Jane Ashford

A SIGNET BOOK

NEW AMERICAN LIBRARY

Ⓢ SIGNET TRADEMARK REG. U.S. PAT. OFF. AND FOREIGN COUNTRIES
REGISTERED TRADEMARK—MARCA REGISTRADA
HECHO EN CHICAGO, U.S.A.

SIGNET, SIGNET CLASSIC, MENTOR, PLUME, MERIDIAN and
NAL BOOKS are published by New American Library
1633 Broadway, New York, New York 10019

First Printing, October, 1984

1 2 3 4 5 6 7 8 9

PRINTED IN THE UNITED STATES OF AMERICA

1

DIANA GRESHAM HUGGED THE THIN COTTON OF HER unadorned nightdress to her chest and snuggled deeper into the pillows of the posting-house bed. She had never been so happy in her life, she told herself, and today was just the beginning of a glorious future. This afternoon, she and Gerald would reach Gretna and be married, and then no one could part them or spoil their wonderful plans—not even her father.

Of course, Papa was unlikely to protest *now*. Diana's lovely face clouded as she considered the terrible step she had been forced to by her father's harshness. If he had only *listened* this once, it wouldn't have been necessary to defy him. But almost eighteen years as Mr. Gresham's sole companion had repeatedly—and painfully—defeated any such hopes. Papa was implacable; he had never shown the least interest in her ideas or opinions, except to condemn them. Diana felt only a small admixture of guilt in her relief at having escaped her rigid, penurious home.

A tap on the door made her expression lighten. Sitting up and smiling expectantly, she called, "Come in." The panels swung back to reveal first a loaded tray, then an extremely handsome young man.

"*Voilà,*" he said, returning her smile possessively. "Tea. And hot toast." He swept a napkin from the tray to display it. "I play servant to you."

Diana clapped her hands. "Thank you! I am so hungry."

"The unaccustomed exertions of the night, no doubt," he replied, placing the tray across her knees and resting a hand on her half-bare shoulder.

Diana flushed fiery red and gazed fixedly at the white teapot. She would get used to such frankness concerning the somewhat discomfiting intimacies of marriage, she thought. Her first experience last night had not been at all like the stolen kisses she and Gerald had exchanged in the weeks since they met. Yet Gerald had obviously seen nothing wrong so Diana dismissed her reaction as naivete. She knew she was much less sophisticated than other girls, even those not yet eighteen. Because her father had never allowed her to attend any party or assembly, nor meet any of the young men who visited her friends' families, Diana was deeply humble about her ignorance, while passionately eager to be rid of it. Until Gerald's miraculous appearance during one of her solitary country walks— an event she still could not help but compare to the illustration of the Archangel Michael in her Bible—she had never spoken to a man of her own age. That her sole opportunity should bring a veritable pink of the ton (a term Gerald had taught her) had been overwhelming. From the first, she had joyfully referred every question to him, and taken his answers as gospel.

Diana raised her eyes, found her promised husband gazing appreciatively at her scantily clad form, and promptly lowered them again.

For his part, Gerald Carshin was congratulating himself on his astuteness. He had been hanging out for a rich wife for nearly ten years, and his golden youth was beginning, however slightly, to tarnish. Even he saw that. His sunny hair remained thick—automati-cally he touched its fashionable perfection—and his light blue eyes had lost none of their dancing charm, but he had started to notice alarming signs of thick-ness in his slim waist and a hint of sag in his smooth cheeks. At thirty, it was high time he wed, and he had cleverly unearthed an absolute peach of an heiress in the nick of time.

Carshin's eyes passed admiringly over Diana's slender rounded form, which was more revealed than hidden by the thin nightdress and coverlet. Her curves were his now; he breathed a little faster thinking of last night. And her face was equally exquisite. Like him, she was blond, but her hair was a deep rich gold, almost bronze, and her eyes were the color of aged sherry, with glints of the same gold in their depths. She wasn't the least fashionable, of course. Her tartar of a father had never allowed her to crop her hair or buy modish gowns. Yet the waves of shining curls that fell nearly to Diana's waist convinced Gerald that there was some substance in the old man's strictures. It had taken his breath away last night when Diana had unpinned her fusty knot and shaken her hair loose.

"Your tea is getting cold," Carshin said indulgently. "I thought you were hungry."

Self-consciously Diana began to eat. She had never breakfasted with a man sitting on her bed—or, indeed, in bed at all until today. But of course, having Gerald there was wonderful, she told herself quickly. Every-thing about her life would be different and splendid now. "Are they getting the carriage ready?" she asked, needing to break the charged silence. "I can dress in a minute."

"There's no hurry." His hand smoothed her fall of hair, then moved to cup a breast and fondle it. "We needn't leave at once." But as he bent to kiss Diana's bare neck, he felt her stiffen. She won't really relax till the knot's tied, he thought, drawing back. A pity she's so young. "Still, when you've finished your tea, you should get up," he added.

Diana nodded, relieved, yet puzzled by her hesitant reaction to Gerald's touch. This was the happiest day of her life, she repeated to herself.

Gerald moved to an armchair by the window. "Once we're married, we'll go straight to London. The season will be starting soon, and I . . . *we* must find a suitable house and furnish it." Gerald pictured himself set up in his own house, giving card parties and taking a box at the opera. How the ton would stare! He would finally have his revenge on the damned high sticklers who cut him.

"Oh, yes," agreed Diana, her breakfast forgotten. "I can hardly wait to see all the fashionable people and go to balls."

Gerald scrutinized her, the visions he had conjured up altering slightly. Diana would of necessity accompany him. "We must get you some clothes first, and do something about your hair." She put a stricken hand to it. "It's lovely, but not quite the thing, you know."

"No." Diana looked worried. "You will tell me how I should go on, and what I am to wear, won't you?"

"Naturally." Gerald seemed to expand in the chair. "We shall be all the crack, you and I. Everyone will invite us."

Diana sighed with pleasure at the thought. All her life she had longed for gaiety and crowds of chattering friends rather than the bleak, dingy walls of her father's house. Now, because of Gerald, she would have them.

"You must write at once to your trustees and tell

them you are married," he added, still lost in a happy dream. "We shall have to draw quite a large sum to get settled in town."

"My trustees?" Diana's brown eyes grew puzzled.

"Yes. You told me their names, but I've forgotten. The banker and the solicitor in charge of your mother's fortune— yours, I should say, now. You come into it when you marry, remember."

"Not unless I am of age," she corrected him.

Gerald went very still. "What?"

"Papa made her put that in. Mr. Merton at the bank told me so. Mama would have left me her money outright, but Papa insisted upon conditions. It is just like him. The money was to be mine when I married, unless I should do so before I came of age. Otherwise, I must wait until I am five-and-twenty. Isn't that infamous?"

Carshin's pale face had gone ashen. "But you are not eighteen for . . ."

"Four months," she finished. Sensing his consternation, she added, "Is something wrong?"

His expression was intent, but he was not looking at her. "We must simply wait to be married," he murmured. "We cannot go to London, of course. We shall have to live very quietly in the country, and—"

"Wait!" Diana was aghast. "Gerald, you promised me we should be married at once. Indeed, I never could have"—she choked on the word "eloped"—"left home otherwise."

Meeting her eyes, Gerald saw unshakable determination, and the collapse of all his careful plans. One thing his rather unconventional life had taught him was to read others' intentions. Diana would not be swayed by argument, however logical.

Why had she withheld this crucial piece of information? he wondered. He had questioned her so carefully.

This was all her fault. In fact, she had neatly trapped him into compromising her. But if she thought that the proprieties weighed with him, she was mistaken. The chit deserved whatever she got.

He looked up, and met her worried gaze. The naked appeal in her dark eyes stopped the flood of recrimination on his tongue, but it did not change his mind. Hunching a shoulder defensively, he rose. "I should see about the horses. You had better get dressed."

"Yes, I will," replied Diana eagerly, relief making her weak. "I won't be a minute."

Gerald nodded curtly, and went out.

But when Diana descended the narrow stair a quarter-hour later, her small valise in her hand, there was no sign of Gerald Carshin. There were only a truculent innkeeper proffering a bill, two sniggering postboys, and a round-eyed chambermaid wiping her hands in her apron.

Diana refused to believe Gerald was gone. Even when it was pointed out that a horse was missing from the stable, along with the gentleman's valise from the hired chaise, Diana shook her head stubbornly. She sat down in the private parlor to await Gerald's return, concentrating all her faculties on appearing unconcerned. But as the minutes ticked past, her certainty slowly ebbed, and after an hour she was trembling under the realization that she had been abandoned far from her home.

Papa had been right. He had said that Gerald wanted nothing but her money. She had thought that his willingness to marry her at seventeen proved otherwise, but she saw now that this wasn't so. Gerald had simply not understood. Hadn't she *told* him all the terms of her mother's will? She thought she had, but her memory of their early meetings was blurred by a romantically golden haze.

It hardly mattered now, in any case. Gerald was gone, and she must think what to do. With shaking fingers Diana opened her reticule and counted the money she had managed to scrape together. Four pounds and seven shillings. It would never be enough to pay the postboys and the inn. She could give them what she had, but where would she go afterward, penniless?

Tears started then, for her present plight and for the ruin of all her hopes and plans. Diana put her face in her hands and sobbed.

It was thus that the innkeeper found her sometime later. He strode into the parlor with an impatient frown, but it faded when he saw Diana's misery. "Here, now," he said, "don't take on so." His words had no discernible effect, and he began to look uneasy. "Wait here a moment until I fetch my wife," he added, backing quickly to the door. Diana paid no heed. She scarcely heard.

A short time later a small plump woman bustled into the room and stood before Diana with her hands on her hips. Her husband peered around the door, but the older woman motioned brusquely for him to shut it, leaving them alone. "Now, miss," she said then, "crying will do you no good, though I can't say as I blame you for it. An elopement, was it?"

Diana cried harder.

The woman nodded. "And your young man has changed his mind seemingly. Well, you've made a bad mistake, no denying that."

Still, the only response was sobs.

"Have you any money at all?"

Diana struggled to control herself. She must make an effort to honor her obligations, however she felt. "F-four pounds," she managed finally, holding out the reticule.

The innkeeper's wife took it and examined the contents. "Tch. The blackguard! He might have left you something more."

"He only cared about getting *my* money," murmured Diana brokenly.

The other's eyes sharpened. "Indeed? Well, miss, my advice is to put him right out of your mind. He's no good."

Diana gazed at the carpet.

"You should go back to your family," added the woman. "They'll stand by you and help scotch the scandal. You haven't been away so very long, I wager."

Diana shuddered at the thought of her father. She couldn't go back to face his contempt. Yet where else could she go?

"Tom and me could advance you some money. Not for a private chaise, mind, but for the stage. You could send it back when you're home again."

"W-would you?" She was amazed.

Something in the girl's tear-drenched brown eyes made the landlady reach out and pat her shoulder. "You'll be all right once you're among your own people again," she said. "But you'd best get ready. The stage comes at ten."

In an unthinking daze, Diana paid the postboys and dismissed them, gathered her meager luggage, and mounted the stage when it arrived. A young man sitting opposite tried to get up a conversation, but Diana didn't even hear him. Her mind was spinning with the events of the past few days. As the miles went by, she recounted them again and again. Why had she not seen Gerald's true colors sooner? Why had she allowed him to cajole her into an elopement? What was to become of her now? She was surely ruined forever through her own foolishness. How could she look anyone in the eye again after what she had done?

Wrapped in these gloomy reflections, Diana was oblivious until the stage set her down at an inn near her home in Yorkshire. And once there, she stood outside the inn's door, her small valise beside her, afraid to reveal her presence.

"Yes, miss, may I help you?" asked a voice, and the innkeeper appeared in the doorway.

Diana tried to speak, and failed.

"Did you want dinner?" he added impatiently. She could hear sounds from the taproom beyond. "Are you waiting for someone to fetch you? Will you come in?"

"No," she answered, her voice very low. "I . . . I am all right. Thank you." She would walk home, she decided. The house was four miles away, but all other alternatives seemed worse.

"Wait a moment. Aren't you the Gresham girl?" The man came out to survey her, and Diana flinched. "I've seen you with your father. They managed to get word to you, then, did they? There was some talk that Mrs. Samuels didn't know where you'd gone."

Diana frowned. Mrs. Samuels was their housekeeper. What did she have to do with anything?

"You'll just be in time for the funeral. It's tomorrow morning. Was you wanting a gig to take you home?"

"Funeral?" she echoed, her lips stiff.

"Well, yes, miss. Your father . . ." Suddenly the innkeeper clapped a hand to his mouth. "You ain't been told! My tongue's run away with me, as usual. Beg your pardon, miss, I'm sure."

"But what has happened? Is my father . . . ?"

The man shook his head. "Passed away late yesterday, miss. And I'm that sorry to tell you. I reckon Mrs. Samuels meant to do it face to face."

"But how?" Diana was dazed by this new disaster.

"Carried off by an apoplexy, they say. A rare temper, Mr. Gresham had . . . er, that is, I've heard folk say so."

He had died of rage at her flight, thought Diana. Not only had she ruined herself, she had killed her father. With a small moan, she sank to the earth in a heap.

The furor that followed did not reach her. Diana was bundled into a gig like a parcel and escorted home by a chambermaid and an ostler. Delivered to Mrs. Samuels and somewhat revived with hot tea, Diana merely stared.

Finally Mrs. Samuels said, "I told them you had gone to visit friends."

Diana choked, then replied, "But you knew . . . I left the note."

"I burned it."

"Why?"

"It was none of their affair, prying busybodies."

The girl gazed at the spare, austere figure of the only mother she had ever known. Her own mother had died when Diana was two, but she had never felt that Mrs. Samuels cared for her. She did not even know her first name. "You lied to protect me?"

The housekeeper's face did not soften, and she continued to stare straight ahead. " 'Twas none of their affair," she repeated. "I don't hold with gossip."

"So no one knows where I went?"

Mrs. Samuels shook her head. "No one asked, save the doctor. The neighbors haven't taken the trouble to call."

And why should they? thought Diana. Her father had had nothing but harsh words for them during his life. Part of the burden lifted from her soul. She still felt ashamed, but at least her shame was private.

"Are you home to stay?" asked Mrs. Samuels, her expression stony.

"I . . . yes."

"And will you be wanting me to stay on?"

Diana stared at her, mystified. The woman had saved her, yet she seemed as devoid of warmth and emotion as ever. If she felt nothing, why had she bothered? What was she thinking? "Of course."

Mrs. Samuels nodded and turned away. "Mr. Gresham is in the front parlor. The funeral is at eleven tomorrow." She left the room with Diana's valise.

Diana hesitated, biting her lower lip. She walked slowly to the closed door of the front parlor, stepped back, then forward. She could not imagine her father dead; his presence had always pervaded this house. Her whole life had been turned upside down in a matter of days, and she was far from assimilating the change. She could not even imagine what it would be like now. Slowly her hand reached out and grasped the door-knob. She took a deep breath and opened the door.

2

ON THE DAY AFTER HER TWENTY-FIFTH BIRTHDAY, Diana Gresham followed a second coffin to the churchyard. Mrs. Samuels had been ill all that winter, and late in February she died, leaving Diana wholly alone. Diana had nursed the old housekeeper faithfully, and she tried to feel some sadness as she stood beside her grave and listened to the rector intone the ritual words, but she could muster no emotion. She and Mrs. Samuels had never been true companions. The closeness that Diana had imagined might come from their shared adversity had never emerged. Indeed, the older woman had merely become more dour and reclusive as the years passed, and Diana had felt increasingly isolated.

When the rector and the few mourners were ready to depart after the brief service, Diana resisted their urgings to come away and wrapped her black cloak more closely around her shoulders as the sexton and his helpers began to fill in the grave. It was a dreary morning, with low gray clouds and a damp bitter chill. Warm weather earlier in the week had turned the winter earth to mud, but there was as yet no hint of green to reconcile one to the dirt. The moors rolling away beyond the stone church were bleak. Yet Diana did not move even when the wind made her cloak billow out around her, bringing the cold to her skin.

She did not want to return to the now empty house, whose cramped rooms were unchanged since her father's death.

For some time, Diana had been feeling restless and dissatisfied. The shocked immobility that had followed her disastrous rebellion seven years before had modulated through remorse and self-loathing into withdrawal, contemplation, and finally, understanding. She had forgiven her younger self a long while ago. Her faults had been great, but they sprang from warmth of feeling and lack of family love rather than weakness. Her mistakes had been almost inevitable, given her naiveté and susceptibility.

But with greater wisdom had also come a loss of the eager openness that the younger Diana had possessed. The habit of solitude had become strong; Diana seldom exchanged more than a few sentences with her scattered neighbors. I am like Mrs. Samuels myself now, she thought, gazing over the moors. I have no friends.

Her restlessness reached a kind of irritated crescendo and she felt she must do something dramatic, or else she would scream. But she did not know what to do. Some change was inevitable. Even had she not been inexpressibly weary of living alone, she could not remain completely solitary. Yet she had no family to take her in. Mr. Merton, the banker, had called yesterday to congratulate her and solemnly explain that she was now in full possession of her fortune. She was a wealthy woman. But she felt resourceless. Money was worse than useless, she realized, if one did not know what to do. Shivering a little as the wind whipped her cloak again, Diana felt she must come to some conclusion before she returned to the house. If she did not, some part of her insisted, she would slip back into her routine of isolation and never break free. She would indeed become a Mrs. Samuels, reluctant to venture beyond her own front door.

I must leave here, she thought, looking from the small churchyard to the narrow village street with its facing rows of stone cottages. All was brown and gray and black; there was no color anywhere. She had never learned to love the harsh landscapes of Yorkshire. But where could she go?

Diana felt a sudden sharp longing for laughter and the sounds of a room full of people. Wistfully she remembered her short time at school. Her father had kept her there less than a year, concluding that she was being corrupted by association with fifty empty-headed girls. Diana recalled their chatter and jokes as part of the happiest time in her life. Her new financial independence would not give her this, however pleasant it might be.

Briefly she was filled with bitterness. It seemed a cruel joke that she should get her fortune now, when events had rendered her incapable of enjoying it. She could buy a house, hire a companion, but she could not regain her old lightheartedness or her girlhood friends. If only her father had been kinder, or Gerald . . . but with this thought, Diana shook her head. She could not honestly blame them for her present plight. Her father had been harsh and distant; Gerald had treated her shamefully. But she herself had repulsed the world in her first remorseful reaction, for no reason that the world could see. Naturally, those she rejected had withdrawn, and it seemed to her now that she had been foolish in this as well as in her rash elopement.

Gathering her cloak, Diana turned and walked through the churchyard gate and along the street toward home. Her father's house, hers now, was beyond the edge of the village, surrounded by high stone walls. As she approached it, Diana walked more slowly, a horror of retreating behind those barriers again growing in her. Was she fated to spoil her life? she wondered.

"Diana. Diana Gresham," called a high, light voice behind her. "Wait, Diana!"

She turned slowly. A small slender woman in a gray cloak and a modish hat was waving from a carriage in the center of the village. Her face was in shadow, and Diana did not recognize her as she got out and hurried forward.

"Oh, lud," she gasped as she came up. "This wind takes my breath away. And I had forgotten the dreadful cold here. But how fortunate to meet you, Diana! Cynthia Addison said you had left Yorkshire, and so I might not even have called! Are you back for a visit, as we are?"

When the woman spoke, Diana recognized Amanda Trent, a friend she had not seen for eight years. Amanda, two years older, had married young and followed her soldier husband to Spain. They had exchanged one or two letters at the beginning, but Amanda was an unreliable correspondent, and Diana had ceased to write after her elopement, as she had ceased to see acquaintances like Cynthia Addison, who could not be blamed for thinking her gone. "Hello, Amanda," she answered, the commonplace words feeling odd on her tongue.

Amanda peered up into her face, sensing some strangeness. She looked just the same, Diana thought —tiny and brunette, with huge almost black eyes. Those eyes had been the downfall of a number of young men before Captain Trent won her hand. "Diana?" Amanda said, a question in her voice.

Making a great effort, Diana replied, "I am not visit-

ing. I never left. After Papa died . . ." She didn't finish
her sentence because the story seemed far too complicated to review; none of the important things could be
told.

Amanda held out both hands. "Yes, they told me
about Mr. Gresham. I am sorry, of course, though . . ."
She shrugged. Long ago, Diana had confided some of
her trials.

Awkwardly Diana took her hands. Amanda
squeezed her fingers and smiled. "Come back with me,
and we shall have a cozy talk. I want to hear everything."

What would she say if she did? wondered Diana, for
Amanda seemed the same gay creature she had been at
nineteen. Yet the chance to put off going home was
irresistible, and shortly they were sitting side by side
in Amanda's carriage riding toward her parents' house
a few miles from the village.

"George is invalided out; he never recovered
properly from the fever he took after Toulouse, so we
decided to come here for a good long visit. I am so
happy to be in England again! You cannot imagine
how inconvenient it sometimes was in Spain, Diana."

Thinking that "inconvenient" was an odd character-
ization of the Pennisular Wars, Diana watched her old
friend's face. Now that they were closer, she could see
small signs of age and strain there. Amanda was no
less pretty, but it was obvious that she was nearly a
decade past nineteen. Her friend's chatter seemed less
carefree, more forced. Diana felt relieved; it had been
daunting to think that only she was altered. "You have
been in Spain all this time?"

"Oh, lud, no! That I *could* not have borne. I spent
two seasons in London, and I was here for the summer
a year ago. I am sorry I did not call, Diana, but I was

. . . ill." She turned her head away. "Here we are. Mama will be so pleased to see you."

Wondering uneasily if this were true, Diana followed Amanda into the house. Mrs. Durham was one of the acquaintances she had ceased to see years ago.

As it happened, none of the family was at home. George Trent was riding with Amanda's father, and Mrs. Durham had gone to visit an ailing tenant rather than share Amanda's drive. The two women settled in the drawing room with a pot of tea and a plate of the spice cakes Diana remembered from childhood visits.

"Are you still in mourning?" asked Amanda then, her expression adding what politeness made her suppress: Diana's clothes and hair were even more unfashionable than before her father's death.

Diana put a hand to the great knot of deep gold at the back of her neck as she explained about Mrs. Samuels. Amanda's dark cropped ringlets and elegant blue morning gown brought back concerns she had not felt for years. The black dress she wore was the last she had bought, for her father's funeral.

Amanda looked puzzled. "But, Diana, what have you been doing all this time? Did you have a London season? Or at least go to York for the winter assemblies?" When Diana shook her head, she opened her eyes very wide. "Do you mean you have just stayed here? But *why?*"

It must indeed seem eccentric, Diana thought, and she could not give her only plausible reason. Her neighbors had probably judged her mad.

Amanda was gazing at her with an unremembered shrewdness. "Is something wrong, Diana? You . . . you seem different. You were always the first to talk of getting away."

Miserably Diana prepared to rise. She could not explain, and Amanda would no doubt take that inability for coldness. Their long-ago friendship was dead.

But Amanda had lapsed into meditative silence. "I suppose we are all changed," she added. "It has been quite a time, after all."

Surprised, Diana said nothing, and in the next moment their tête-à-tête was interrupted by the entrance of Amanda's family.

The Durhams were familiar, though Diana had not seen them recently, and their greetings were more cordial than she had expected. They did not mention her strange behavior or seem to see anything odd in her sudden visit to their house. But as they spoke, Diana gradually received the impression that they were too preoccupied with more personal concerns to think of her.

One cause, at least, was obvious. Diana had never seen a greater alteration in a person than in George Trent, Amanda's husband. She remembered him as a smiling blond giant, looking fully able to toss his tiny bride high in the air and catch her again without the least strain. Now, after seven years in the Peninsula, he retained only his height. His once muscular frame was painfully thin; his bright hair and ruddy complexion were dulled, and he wore a black patch over one blue eye. Diana's presence appeared to startle and displease him, though he said nothing, merely retreating to the other side of the room and pretending interest in an album that lay on a table. His family watched him anxiously but covertly.

"George," said Amanda finally, when his conduct was becoming rude, "you remember Diana Gresham. She was at our wedding, and I have spoken to you of her."

George was very still for a moment; then he turned,

squaring his shoulders as if to face an ordeal. "Miss Gresham," he said, bowing his head slightly.

"Doesn't George look dashing and romantic?" Amanda continued, her tone rather high and brittle. "I tell him he is positively piratical and he must take care not to set too many hearts aflutter, or I shall be dreadfully jealous. Don't I, George?"

"Me and everyone else," he replied, and strode abruptly out of the room.

Amanda made a small sound, and when Diana turned she saw that her eyes were filled with tears. She felt sharp pity and fear that she intruded.

"It was only a tiny wound," said Amanda shakily. "But they could not save his eye. And then he took the fever as well. I had hoped that being home again would be good for George, but he doesn't seem to want to recover."

"You've been here only a week, Amanda," answered Mr. Durham. "Give him time."

"Yes, darling." Amanda's mother looked as if she might cry too. "I'm sure it is very hard for him, but he will come round."

Diana rose. "Perhaps I should take my leave."

The Durhams exchanged a glance.

"Please don't," cried Amanda. Then, realizing that she had spoken too fervently, added, "I beg your pardon. Why should you wish to stay, after all? It is just that I have been so . . ." She broke off and dropped her head in her hands.

Diana moved without thinking to sit beside her friend and put an arm around her shoulders. "Of course I will stay if you wish it. I feared I was prying into private matters."

"George does not allow it to be private." Amanda's voice was muffled. "I am selfish to keep you, Diana. It was just so splendid to see someone from the old days." She raised her head. "The things we remember of each other are so . . . simple."

It was true, Diana thought, and the thought appealed to her as much as it did Amanda. Whatever worries each might have, between them there was nothing but pleasant recollections. Here was an opportunity to end her loneliness without explanations or the great effort of finding and cultivating new acquaintances. At long last, fate seemed to be coming to her aid. "I should like to stay," she said. "I should like it very much."

Amanda met her eyes, and for a moment they gazed at one another as two women, a little buffeted by the world and sadder and wiser than the girls they had been when they last met. A flash of wordless communication passed between them; then Amanda smiled and clasped her hands. "I'm so glad. We will have another cup of tea and talk of all our old friends. Do you know what has become of Sophie Jenkins?"

Returning her smile, Diana shook her head.

"She married an earl!"

"But she wished to become a missionary!"

"So she always *said*. But when she got to London, she threw that idea to the winds and pursued a title until she snared one. They say her husband is a complete dunce."

Diana couldn't help but laugh, and Amanda's mischievous grin soon turned to trilling laughter as well. They both went on a bit longer than the joke warranted, savoring the sensation.

"I hope you will stay to dinner, Diana," said Mrs. Durham then. "I know you are alone now."

Diana had nearly forgotten the older couple. Turning quickly, she saw encouraging smiles on both their faces. "I should like that. Thank you." Did they really want her? she wondered.

"That's right!" Amanda's dark eyes widened as she thought of something. "Diana! You must come and stay here. You cannot live alone, and I should adore having you. Wouldn't we, Mama?"

"Of course."

Mrs. Durham did not sound as enthusiastic as her daughter, thought Diana. But neither did she seem insincere. Suddenly the idea was very attractive. She would not have to go back to that dreary house for a while; she could put off the decision about what to do. Yet the habit of years was strong. "I don't know . . ." she began.

"You must come," urged Amanda. "We shall have such fun." Tension was in her voice, and Diana could not resist her plea. She nodded, and Amanda embraced her exuberantly.

"For a few days," murmured Diana, her eyes on the Durhams.

But the older couple watched their daughter with pleased relief.

And so it was that Diana closed up her father's house on the day after Mrs. Samuels' funeral and settled into a pleasant rose-papered bedchamber at the Durhams'. The room was much more comfortable than her own, and she was unused to a large staff of servants. Diana had dismissed all the servants but Mrs. Samuels after her father's death, doing the household chores as a kind of penance. She now realized that she had never learned to enjoy the work, and she saw no further need to punish herself.

As the days passed it became more and more obvious that Diana's presence was good for Amanda, and Diana took this as reason enough for the

Durhams' kindness. That the opposite was also true, she did not consider for some time. Yet at the end of the first week, Diana realized that she was happier than she had been for months, perhaps years. Amanda's companionship filled a great void in her life, and a more luxurious style of living suited her completely.

At the beginning of Diana's second week at the Durhams', as she and Amanda walked together on a balmy March afternoon, Amanda said, "We are the only two of our friends who have stayed the same, or nearly the same, anyway. I have seen Sophie and Jane and Caroline in town, and they are all vastly changed. They talk of people I don't know, and they seem wrapped up in town life. I suppose it is because you and I were cut off from society."

"Did you see no one in Spain?" Diana was curious about her friend's experiences abroad, though she did not wish to bring forth any painful memories.

"Some other officers' wives, but they were often posted away just as we became friendly. And I never got on with the Spanish and Portugese ladies." She sighed. "George was most often with the army, of course. I spent a great deal of time alone."

"You came back for visits." Diana wondered why she had not stayed in England, as most army wives did.

"Yes. But then I missed George so dreadfully." Amanda's smile was wry. "We were . . . *are* so fond of one another. It is very unfashionable."

"I remember when you met him. One day you were perfectly normal, then you went to an assembly in York and came back transformed. We could hardly force a sentence from you. It took days to discover what was the matter."

Amanda laughed. "We were both bowled over. We married six weeks later."

"And the rest of us nearly died of jealousy."

They laughed. But Amanda's expression soon sobered again. "And now we are all scattered—Sophie in Kent, Jane in Dorset, and Caroline flitting from London to Brighton to house parties. It all seems so long ago." She paused. "Of course, they all have children, too. It makes them seem older."

Diana sensed constraint. "When you and George are settled . . ." she began.

Amanda shook her head as if goaded. "I have lost three. I . . . I don't hope . . . that is . . ." She bit her lower lip and struggled for composure. "But what am I about, discussing such things with you? An unmarried girl! Mama would be scandalized." She paused again, taking a deep breath. "You know what we must do, Diana? We must find you a husband. You are . . . what? —five-and-twenty? Nearly on the shelf. How careless of you!" Abruptly her eyes widened. "I did not mean . . . Oh, I haven't offended you, have I? My tongue runs away with me sometimes."

"Of course you have not." But Diana did feel uneasy. "I have never had the opportunity to marry. I don't suppose I shall." Even if I did have the chance, she thought, no one would marry me once they learned of my past. Diana knew she could never keep such a secret from a husband.

"Nonsense." Amanda examined her friend with a more critical eye than she had used so far. Diana had been very pretty at seventeen; now, her color was not so good, admittedly, but her deep golden hair had lost none of its vibrancy, and the unfashionable way she dressed it was somehow very attractive. Her face was thinner, but her brown eyes with gold flecks remained entrancing. Her form was slender and pleasing, even in the poorly cut black. Amanda's own dark eyes began to sparkle. It was unthinkable that Diana should not marry, and this was just the sort of problem that appealed to her. A keen interest that Amanda had not felt for some time rose in her, temporarily banishing worry. How could her plan be best accomplished? Slowly an idea started to form, which, she reasoned, might work for George as well.

3

"I THINK," DECLARED AMANDA TRENT AT DINNER that evening, "that we should go to Bath for a long visit." Four pairs of eyes focused on her face. Her parents were obviously surprised, and not overpleased. Diana looked dismayed, and George antagonistic. Amanda's pointed chin rose. "I don't know why I did not think of it before," she continued. "It would be a perfect holiday for us. We don't want the hurly-burly of London, yet the country is a bit flat at this season. So . . ."

"I am *not* an invalid," interrupted George through clenched teeth.

A flicker of pain, instantly suppressed, clouded Amanda's dark eyes. "An invalid?" she repeated, as if mystified. "But of course you are not. What has that to do with anything?"

Confused by his wife's bland innocence, Major Trent blinked. He was, he knew, all too likely to lose his temper these days. He tried to control his irritation, but rarely succeeded. In fact, he hadn't been himself since he had taken that damned fever. But he wasn't to be cajoled into coddling himself and drinking "medicinal" waters. Death in the field was preferable to life as a bleating invalid.

"I only thought you would enjoy seeing old friends," Amanda said, her tone reproachful. "You know that a

great many of them went to Bath. You could ride with
them and discuss all the news. The papers would come
sooner there, you know. You would hear what Wellington is doing in Vienna almost as soon as it happens.
And there would be concerts and assemblies in the
evening, which I should enjoy." Without seeming to,
she watched his face anxiously. It was vital to
convince George; the others presented no obstacle if he
could be brought to agree. And once in Bath, among
friends in some cases more seriously wounded than he,
surely George could be brought to take more care of
himself, and mend the faster.

Major Trent gazed at his still-full plate, a wave of
guilt sweeping over him. It could not be very amusing
for Amanda to be saddled with such a husband as he
had been these past months. She deserved some diversion. And though this thought merely irritated him the
more—for his condition was not his fault—he grunted
assent. "If you wish it."

Amanda asked for no more. She had not hoped for
even grudging agreement so quickly. "We will go as
soon as may be," she replied. "Perhaps by the end of
this week. Do you care to come, Mama, Papa? We
should be happy to have your company."

Mrs. Durham knew what her daughter was doing,
and she approved. George would be far happier among
his own friends, and the entertainments of Bath would
keep him from brooding over his loss. Yet she hated to
send Amanda off alone with her radically altered husband. He was so difficult now, she thought, and
despite her experiences, Amanda was still so young.
But she herself had responsibilities that could not be
lightly pushed aside. As she started to speak, Mr.
Durham said, "I do not see how I can go away just
now, Amanda. We are trying a new method of draining

the Huddleston fields, and I don't trust Bains to oversee repair of the tenant cottages. He is too likely to use inferior materials. But you might go, Celia." He exchanged a concerned look with his wife.

"I suppose I could," answered Mrs. Durham slowly.

Amanda laughed, knowing their thoughts. "There is not the least need, if you do not wish to go. I know you are both happiest here. We shall be very well entertained in Bath."

"I do not like to send you off alone," murmured her mother, hoping this would not provoke one of George's outbursts.

"But I shall not be alone," exclaimed Amanda. "Diana will be there." Seeing everyone's surprise, she spread her hands. "But of course Diana must come. I always meant her to. What would she do here in Yorkshire, without anyone?"

Diana, who had been listening with increasing unhappiness to Amanda's plans, felt a great flood of relief. The prospect of returning to her empty house had been even more distressing after her pleasant interlude with the Durhams. But she felt obliged to say, "I shall be quite all right. You needn't invite me because . . ."

"Oh, Diana, you will not desert me now, surely?" wailed her friend. "We have had such fun together. And think how lovely it will be in Bath."

Diana did think. The idea was immensely attractive. "I don't wish to be in the way," she said reluctantly, glancing at George.

"Don't be silly. George will disappear with his friends to discuss politics, and I shall be left alone for hours. You must bear me company."

"Good thought," grunted George.

Though his tone was sullen, this was the greatest

approval Diana had heard him express during her visit. Gratefully she capitulated. "I should love to come with you."

"Splendid!" Amanda smiled and clasped her hands. "We need only pack our things, then, and we can be off. I daresay we can start in two days' time."

In the event, it took them two weeks to make ready. George discovered some business matters concerning his nearby estate which needed his attention. Mr. Durham managed the property for him, but there were decisions that only George could make, and he found it necessary to visit some of the tenants in order to resolve all the problems. Diana decided to put her father's house, and nearly everything it contained, up for sale. She sorted through all her possessions and packed them up, arranging for an agent to watch over the place and handle its sale. She also called at the bank and learned exactly what her new financial status was. She and Mr. Merton determined an income, to be paid to her quarterly, and the firm gladly agreed to watch over the principal for the time being.

On the day Diana left her family's home for the last time, her clothes and personal items tied up and ready to be delivered to the Durhams', she walked through the rooms and tried to distinguish some scraps of regret among her feelings. She could not. As a child here, she had felt her natural exuberance repressed; as a young girl, she had longed only to leave; and in the last few years, she had labored under the oppression of her own mistakes and misfortunes. She would miss nothing in these now dusty and forlorn apartments.

Her certainty was both liberating and frightening. She could start afresh without guilt, but to have so little past—no one and no place to come back to— shook her to the depths. Her life was truly hers alone.

What could she make of it? Her early efforts had been disastrous. Was she any more prepared to go forth now than she had been at seventeen?

Of course she was, Diana told herself, holding her head high. She had to be; the years she had spent pondering had given her wisdom. However, as she followed the carters carrying the last of her trunks and locked the oaken front door behind them, she felt a quiver of apprehension. Perhaps she should have retreated to her old home after all, where all was familiar, if unexciting. At least here she had known who she was. Diana stood still, one hand flat against the wood, then shook her head decisively and turned away.

On her return to the Durhams', Diana found the whole household in an uproar. The contrast to her own silent home was dizzying, and for a moment she could only stand amazed in the front hall, and listen to Mr. Durham and George Trent debating loudly in the library, Mrs. Durham calling to her daughter upstairs, and excited talk floating up from the servants' quarters below. Then she recovered and hurried up to Amanda.

"Oh, Diana!" the latter exclaimed when she entered. "Did you hear the news? Napoleon has escaped St. Helena and is marching through France gathering a new army. Wellington is recalled from the Congress. It will be war again."

Diana took this in.

"George is frantic to leave. Thank heaven we are nearly ready. I had to argue for an hour against going straight to London. He hates it there, and he will get the papers nearly as quickly in Bath."

"Is he . . . will he go back into the army?"

"Oh, no. He is not completely recovered. And he is

mustered out." Amanda grimaced. "Do not tell, but I am glad."

Diana nodded, understanding.

"Have you finished packing?"

"Yes. I shut the house."

"Good. I expect we shall go tomorrow. Lud, I thought we were finished with this war."

Diana, feeling very ignorant, nodded again. She had never paid proper attention to such important matters, she thought.

They set off for Bath on a fine day in late March, Diana and Amanda in a post chaise, and George Trent riding beside, having gruffly refused his wife's plea to join them and help relieve the tedium of the journey. Diana, knowing that her friend wished to lessen her husband's exertions, had added her arguments, but to no avail. The roads were still deep in mud, but the weather was much warmer, and they made slow but steady progress southward, driven by George's impatience. Aside from frequent anxious glances out the window, Amanda was content, and Diana found herself more and more attached to her old friend as they endured the vicissitudes of travel together. For the first time, she began to understand how Amanda had borne years abroad and the numberless inconveniences inevitable in military lodgings: no setback seemed to worry or discourage Amanda Trent. If a horse went lame or a posting house had nothing to offer but bread, cheese, and ale for their dinner, she accepted it with cheerful optimism, insisting that things would soon be better and raising everyone else's spirits with some anecdote of far more harrowing conditions in Spain. Only her husband's moods and misfortunes could depress her, Diana saw now; she had not realized this until they were on the road and other difficulties arose. She marveled at the depth of love Amanda must feel, to be so solicitous. She herself more than once stifled a sharp retort when George Trent was particularly gruff or truculent.

March was ending by the time they reached Bath, and daffodils were showing by the side of the road. Diana was very glad when they reached the final stage, and the postboys informed them that they would arrive in the city by midafternoon. She was heartily sick of the bouncing chaise, ill-aired inn sheets, and the effort to appear good-humored for every minute of the day. She was addicted to a certain amount of solitude, she found, and though she was fonder than ever of Amanda, she nevertheless wished they might escape each other for some part of the day—as they would, of course, in Bath.

They drove into the town at three on a cloudless afternoon and went directly to the Royal Crescent, where Amanda had engaged a set of apartments. As they passed through the streets, the ladies commented on the beauties of the place. Diana had never seen Bath, and Amanda had not visited for some years.

"How lovely," exclaimed Diana as they pulled up before their lodgings. The pale buildings of the crescent curved before them, overlooking a wide sloping lawn with the garden below.

"You won't mind the hill, will you?" Amanda asked as both women descended from the post chaise. "I tried to find rooms farther down, but there was nothing suitable. We can always hire a chair."

"Why, it's nothing at all," replied Diana, looking back at the steep slant they had ascended. "I can walk that easily. How beautiful it all is. I can never thank you properly for asking me to come, Amanda."

"Nonsense. I should have been sadly flat without you. And here is the building, number five. I do hope they had my last letter."

All was well within, the rooms ready and quite satisfactory. As the servants carried their things inside and began to unpack, Diana and Amanda went through the apartments together and exclaimed at the elegance of the furnishings. Amanda repeatedly called her husband's attention to some particularly fine detail. "If only we could have found such lodgings in Spain, George," she laughed finally, when they had gathered in the drawing room and she no longer had to shout down the stairs to capture his attention. "Do you remember our first place in Madrid? I should have thought I was in heaven if I had walked in here then."

Diana was surprised at George Trent's reminiscent smile. "Still, we had some fine times there. Remember the night Johnny Eagleton came to dinner?" George asked.

Amanda laughed. "Do I not!" She turned to Diana. "He brought his own goose, alive, and expected me to cook it for him. I had only a Spanish girl of fourteen to help me—we could scarcely speak four words to one another—and here was this great bird flapping and hissing about the drawing room. And George would do nothing but laugh!"

He laughed now, for the first time since Diana had met him again. "I wonder where Johnny is now? I suppose he is with the army in America." At this thought, his smile faded again, and he turned away.

"Are you going out to gather news?" asked Amanda, keeping her tone resolutely gay. "If you pass the assembly rooms, you must put our names down. I daresay you will see a dozen acquaintances in the street. Or in the Pump Room. We must ask what is the fashionable hour there."

Major Trent did not reply, but his attention seemed caught, and in a few minutes he did indeed go out.

"Oh, I do hope he encounters some old friends," said Amanda, watching him from the drawing-room window. "It will make such a difference."

"I'm sure he will," replied Diana. "I saw uniforms everywhere as we drove in."

"Yes, a great many men are still in the army," Amanda said, though she was distracted, her eyes still on her husband.

Diana wished to offer Amanda some diversion, but her mind held only envy of the major. She longed to go exploring herself.

At last Amanda turned from the panes. "I believe I will go upstairs and lie down. I am tired out from the journey."

Diana had rather hoped they could go out together, but she merely said, "Of course. Can I do anything for you?"

"No." Amanda smiled. "If you would like to see the town, you could take one of the maids."

Diana's answering smile was sheepish, and her friend laughed. "Go on. I can see you are longing to get out."

"It is just that I have never visited such a place before," apologized Diana. "You are a jaded traveler."

As always, Amanda remembered her friend's sheltered history with a start. When one talked with Diana, it was so easy to forget that she had never been anywhere or done anything, because she seemed so knowledgeable. "Go, by all means," Amanda urged, "only keep Fanny with you and do not get lost."

Fanny was the Yorkshire girl they had hired as
Diana's personal maid.

"Yes, Mama," laughed Diana. "And I shall be home
in time for tea."

"See that you are," responded the other with mock
severity. They walked up the stairs arm in arm, laughing together, so that Diana could fetch her hat.

Diana found the town fascinating. Never in her life
had she been able to stroll through bustling streets and
observe such a variety of people. Though she stopped
nowhere, she paused before the exclusive shops in
Milsom Street, the desire for a new wardrobe rising in
her breast, and she gazed at the Pump Room and the
assembly rooms with eager eyes. Despite her good
looks, she herself was not much marked because of her
unfashionable black gown and outmoded bonnet, but
this suited Diana perfectly. She would not have known
how to turn away excessive interest. As it was, she
could revel in the novel sights and sounds of Bath
secure under the meager protection of Fanny, whose
eyes and mouth were so wide she continually tripped
over her own feet.

The afternoon waned, and Diana reluctantly concluded that it was time to turn toward their lodgings.
She consoled herself with the knowledge that she was
actually staying in town, and that she might take such
a walk every day if she chose, as well as attend the
public concerts and assemblies. The prospect sent her
into a happy daze of anticipation.

Thus, neither Diana nor Fanny was watching very
carefully as they made their way along the pavement
in the general direction of the Royal Crescent. Town
dwellers might have warned them that the street was
no place for pleasant imaginings, particularly in early

spring when the dirt was greatest, but they were not acquainted with any Bath resident, and none was likely to accost a stranger with unsolicited advice.

They turned into one of the major thoroughfares and, skirting a wide puddle, went on toward home. Diana did not even turn her head at the clatter of hooves and wheels behind; the approach of a carriage had already become commonplace, though she would have run to the window in excitement just a week before, at home.

The noise intensified and someone shouted, "Look out, there!" With a sudden rush, a hired chaise swept around the corner and cut through the broad puddle in the road, throwing up a spray of mud and water nearly six feet high. Diana and Fanny were directly in its path; in an instant, they were coated from head to foot with mud. There was not even time to throw up an arm to protect their faces.

Diana was so startled that she did not move for a moment; then she raised a hand to her face and wiped ineffectually at the stiffening mask. "Pull up, you fool!" she heard a male voice shout. She blinked her eyes rapidly, a speck of mud making them water, and tried to focus as the tall figure in uniform rapidly approached. "I *beg* your pardon," said the same voice. "That idiot of a driver didn't see you, I suppose. Are you all right? Apart from this confounded mud, of course."

Diana peered up at him, her vision still clouded. He wore the dark blue jacket and gray trousers of the Royal Horse Guards, the red and gold trim seeming painfully bright in her present condition. But though his uniform was smart, he looked thin for his height, his broad shoulders a little too wide for his girth, and his face showed signs of hardship and suffering. He couldn't be more than thirty, she thought, but he had certainly seen a good deal of action.

The man smiled, and his thin face was abruptly transformed. He was by no means unhandsome, but his brown hair and light blue eyes were not really striking until he smiled. His gaze seemed to take light from the air, and the planes of his high cheekbones shifted to reveal a character and temperament more attractive than mere good looks. He laughed, and this impression intensified. Diana felt an odd fluttering near the base of her throat. "I *am* sorry," he added. "I am not laughing at you, you know. It is just . . ."

" . . . that I look so very ridiculous," finished Diana, imagining her eyes looking out of a mud-covered face. Her tone was sharp, though she did not precisely blame him for the incident. He had not been driving, after all, and he had apologized. Yet she could not help but be irritated.

"Not at all." But his blue eyes danced. "Allow me to make amends by driving you home. It is the least I can do."

"We will muddy your carriage," answered Diana, who nonetheless had no intention of refusing his offer.

"It is hired, and no more than the driver deserves, for his carelessness." He started to offer his arm, then thought better of it, his smile widening.

"I ought to insist upon support," responded Diana, ruthlessly suppressing an answering smile at the thought of how his smart uniform sleeve would look covered with mud.

At once, he extended his arm again. "You are welcome to it."

She shook her head and stepped toward the chaise. "I could not spoil your uniform."

"It has seen worse than mud." His expression was wry as he turned to follow her. He had a cane and walked with one stiff knee, Diana noticed. "And I shall be putting it off for a time here in Bath, worse luck."

"You are on leave?"

He nodded as he put a hand under her elbow to help her into the carriage. "At the worst possible time, naturally." He ushered Fanny into the forward seat and climbed in after her, his stiff left leg making his movement awkward. "My name is Robert Wilton, by the by. Which way?"

Diana gave her direction and sat back. Her initial anger at the accident was fading, only to be replaced by a far more intense chagrin at the manner of their meeting. She found Robert Wilton extremely engaging. Why could she not have encountered him in the assembly rooms, or the concert hall, when she had acquired a new gown and perhaps a modicum of assurance? Diana knew she would never match the London misses who had had the benefit of a season and constant practice in the art of conversation, but she might have made a better impression than this. She fingered her mud-stiffened black gown. He could not even have a proper idea of what she looked like, and he must think her a perfect fool for being caught so.

Yet why did it matter what he thought, Diana wondered? She knew nothing of him. Was she so susceptible that she swooned over the first male she met after years of solitude? Diana flushed crimson at the thought. She had made that mistake before; had she learned nothing since then? Setting her jaw, she gazed out the window at the passing scene.

"Are you *very* angry?" asked Wilton. "I cannot blame you, of course, but I do hope you will get over it." He paused, as if waiting for something, then added, "Will you tell me your name, though I do not deserve it?"

Realizing that she should have done so when he gave his, she said, "Diana Gresham," in a stiff voice.

"You are staying in Bath?"

"Yes." Why did he insist on talking? she wondered, longing to escape.

"I, too. Perhaps we shall meet again." Again he waited, a bit puzzled. She had seemed so open at first, and he had been deeply impressed by her reaction to the accident. Most women, he imagined, would have collapsed in a fit of the vapors and screeched at him like a fishwife. Miss Gresham had not only remained calm, she had traded a mild joke with him. What had he done to turn her so cold?

Robert Wilton was the first to admit that he knew nothing of women. For the six years since he came of age, he had been fighting with Wellington's army. He had not spent more than a score of evenings in a drawing room in his life, and he was always deucedly awkward with the girls his mother put in his way on those occasions. His eldest brother, Lord Faring, rallied him about it whenever they met. Yet with this woman, Wilton had felt no constraint at first. Probably he had put his foot in it somehow, without even knowing it, he thought. He would drop her at her lodgings and fade away as quickly as possible. But this thought brought an immediate protest from some part of him, and he found himself asking, "You are here with your parents?" At least he would know what name to seek, he thought.

"No, with friends." Diana's tone was discouraging. She would not make an even greater fool of herself, she thought. But when silence descended upon the carriage, she felt a pang of regret. They were nearly at the crescent. In a moment, she would climb down, and the incident would be closed forever. "Major and Mrs. Trent," she heard herself add.

"*George* Trent?"

"Yes."

"But we are old friends. Has he recovered from the fever he took at Toulouse?"

"Not . . . not completely," faltered Diana.

"I must call at once." They pulled up before the house, and he jumped out to help Diana, wincing as his stiff knee jarred against the cobblestones. It seemed he was actually coming in with her. Diana searched her mind for a deterrent, but it turned out to be unnecessary. "Please convey my compliments and say I shall come soon, perhaps tomorrow."

Diana nodded.

"And, again, my deepest apologies." He bowed slightly.

She nodded again and turned toward the door.

"George will tell you that mud is my natural element," added Wilton, laughter in his voice.

When she looked over her shoulder, he was getting back into the carriage. Inexplicably, Diana felt a pang of misery. Why must she botch everything? she wondered. She resolved to be a paragon of polish and elegance when Robert Wilton called on the Trents.

4

WILTON DID NOT CALL THE FOLLOWING DAY, A FACT
which filled Diana with profound gratitude. The slight
pique she felt at his omission was overwhelmed by the
memory of Amanda's peals of laughter when she had
entered the house covered with mud. Despite valiant
efforts to control herself, Amanda had been helpless
with mirth for quite five minutes, and this measure of
her appearance had made Diana all the more
determined to smarten it.

Early that morning the two of them had set out on a
lengthy shopping expedition, returning with two
gowns that Diana could wear with only small altera-
tions and the satisfaction of having ordered a great
many more. She had also equipped herself with new
gloves, hats, and other necessities, to the immense
gratification of numerous Milsom Street shopkeepers.
There remained only one great question in the matter
of toilette.

"I suppose I must cut my hair," said Diana, criti-
cally evaluating her image in her dressing-table mirror.
The great knot of deep gold low on her neck seemed in-
congruous with the new blue muslin dress she was
wearing.

Amanda, who had accompanied her to her bedchamber, got up and walked all around Diana, her dark
eyes narrow with speculation. "I don't know. Your hair

is not the latest thing, of course, but it is somehow right on you."

Diana laughed. "I am a hopeless dowd, you mean."

"Not at all! You are just . . . yourself."

"And how am I to take that?" Her expression was wry. "Is not everyone? And is 'myself' so outmoded?"

"I am not saying it properly." Amanda surveyed her friend's tall willowy figure, lovely in the draped muslin. It was so lucky that the dressmaker had had this model made up. The deep vibrant blue, against Diana's bronze hair and pale skin, transformed her from a commonplace pretty girl into a beauty who drew one's eyes and fixed it. Her sherry-colored glance seemed brighter, and even her smile was now dazzling rather than merely pleasant. The unusual knot of hair seemed to confirm her compelling individuality, emphasizing the intelligence and discernment visible in her face and warning observers that here was no milk-and-water miss such as they might meet twenty times a day. Amanda felt it would be wrong to change that, but she did not know how to convey her intuition.

"I admit I am reluctant to cut it," added Diana, turning her head to look at her hair. She too felt some intimation of rightness.

"How long is it now?"

"Nearly to my knees!" She laughed. "Horridly countrified."

"Let us leave it for now," decided Amanda. "You can always have it cut off, but once it is gone . . ." She shrugged.

Diana gave a small involuntary shiver. "Yes." She held out the skirt of her gown and turned to look at the back in the mirror. "How splendid it is to have a new dress. Perhaps I shall become utterly improvident and order a dozen more tomorrow."

Amanda laughed. "Do. And you must wear that one to the concert tonight. You look beautiful!"

Diana threw back her head and drew in a breath. The image her mirror showed her *was* gratifying and far removed from the mud-plastered apparition of yesterday. Captain Wilton—as Amanda had labeled him—was in for a surprise.

"Robert Wilton will never know you again," said Amanda, uncannily echoing this thought.

"If he is there," replied Diana with airy unconcern.

Amanda eyed her. She had been very interested to hear of Diana's encounter. Though not, of course, precisely what she had had in mind when she suggested the stay in Bath (she suppressed a smile), the meeting was nonetheless a beginning. And Captain Wilton was just the sort of man she would have Diana meet. She had been careful to drop only a few scraps of information about him, and she was gratified to see Diana transparently disguising a strong interest. She decided to make another test. "Oh, I daresay he will be. Robert will be very bored on leave and eager for diversion."

Diana studiously examined the line of her hem. "Is he so jaded?"

"Oh, no. Quite the opposite. He has been in the army since he was very young, and had few opportunities for entertainment."

"He was in the Peninsula with George?"

"Yes. That is, not *with* him exactly. Robert was attached to the headquarters staff. He visited all the regiments at one time or another, carrying messages or observing. Which is not to say that he did not see a good deal of action, for he did. I believe he received a special commendation at Salamanca."

"Ah." Diana turned, gown forgotten. "He looked ill. Or, not ill precisely, but worn down."

"He was wounded at Bordeaux, I think, after we had come home. Does he seem very bad?"

Flushing a little, Diana retreated again. "I know nothing of him, of course. I thought he was a little thin and pale, and his leg is stiff."

Amanda nodded wisely. "That does not sound too serious. But if he is still on leave, it must have been. I suppose he is as wild to rejoin Wellington as they all are."

"Has he no . . . family?" asked Diana haltingly.

"Oh, lud, yes. He is the brother of Lord Faring and has several sisters. His father is dead, but Lady Faring, his mother, is quite a figure in London—one of the leading hostesses."

"I wonder he does not stay with her."

"Perhaps Faring puts him off. He is a dreadful dandy." She giggled. "You should see him, Diana. He cannot turn his head, his collar is so high and starched, and his waist is cinched so small he is shaped like an hourglass."

"Ridiculous," she agreed, "but hardly enough to put one off London, I should think."

"Oh, but he is—they are, I mean. Most of the military men can't abide dandies, or the haut ton, because they were all so stupid about the war, you see. They acted as if it were unimportant. George calls them—what is the word—fribbles." She giggled again. "When he is in a *kind* mood, that is."

Diana smiled. "It is lucky we came to Bath, then. The town seems full of soldiers."

"Luck had nothing to do with it."

Her smug tone made Diana look more closely.

Amanda had schemes in mind, she saw, and she
suddenly wondered if some of them might not involve
herself. The idea startled her, for the Amanda Diana
remembered would have had little time for or interest
in maneuvering others. Diana could see how George's
state might alter this, but what else was Amanda plotting? This question, presently unanswerable, was unsettling.

That evening, they attended a concert in the lower
rooms. Diana had thought that George Trent would
refuse to come, but he said nothing and seemed
content when they met him in the drawing room and
walked downstairs together. He had been much less
prickly since they arrived in Bath, Diana realized. He
still looked like a ghost of his former self, his massive
frame barely covered by his flesh and his face thin and
lined behind the black eyepatch. But his temper was
improved, and when they entered the concert room,
she understood at least part of the reason. George was
greeted from all sides by men like himself—soldiers
discharged from Wellington's army. He fell
immediately into intent conversation about recent
developments, leaving Diana and Amanda to find their
own seats among the rows of gilt chairs. Neither had
the slightest objection, however. Indeed, Diana could
see that Amanda was overjoyed at her husband's re-
kindled animation, and she herself felt happy for both
of them.

Diana looked about the room with interest, sitting
very straight, conscious for almost the first time in her
life that she looked well-dressed and elegant. Amanda
had lent her a string of pearls to wear with her new
blue gown; a fringed shawl was draped across her
elbows, and she carried a pair of gloves she had

purchased that day. As the hall filled and the murmur of talk grew louder, Diana felt her heartbeat quicken. Society was what she had longed for so ardently years ago. Her chance had come when she had almost given up hope, and she was terribly excited.

Amanda had been nodding to the left and right, smiling and occasionally raising her hand in greeting. "I had no notion we would find so many acquaintances here," she said. "Half the army seems to be in Bath. I had supposed most were in America. Why, there is Anthony Linton!"

"I don't see nearly as many uniforms as on the street," commented Diana.

"Those must be the new arrivals. They don't wear uniforms once on leave, of course."

Diana assimilated this information. She had, she realized, been covertly on the lookout for a blue coat trimmed with red and gold.

"George knows everyone much better than I, naturally," continued Amanda. "But it is very pleasant to have even a nodding acquaintance with so many. It makes one feel at home."

Diana, who had begun to feel just the opposite, scanned the room again. It was filled with strangers— far more men than women—talking in small earnest groups.

At the signal, the audience settled into chairs, and after a short interval the music began.

Diana, who had never been musical, found the performance merely pleasant, and from the looks of the other listeners, she thought that many would concur. The rush to resume conversation or visit the refreshment room at the first pause was marked. She and Amanda were swept along irresistibly and had some difficulty in procuring glasses of lemonade and chairs at one of the small tables. Her unconcern at George's desertion wavered a bit, as did her elation at being out. Then, at that inauspicious moment, Diana saw Robert Wilton making his way through the crowd around the entrance to the refreshment room. At once, her interest revived. He wore a plain blue coat tonight and buff pantaloons, and he carried an ebony cane upon which he occasionally leaned when someone accidentally jostled him and threw him onto his stiff knee. He was gazing at the various groups of people, and Diana sat a little straighter, waiting for his eyes to encounter hers.

They did so, and passed on without a flicker. She frowned, then realized that he could not be expected to recognize her without the mud. Her lips curved upward at the absurdity of it. How were they to meet? Forgetting her earlier scruples, she turned to Amanda. "There is Captain Wilton."

"Where?" Diana indicated him. "So it is." Amanda raised a hand and, when she managed to catch his eye, nodded and smiled. Robert Wilton immediately started toward them, though his progress was slow because of the crush.

"Mrs. Trent," he said when he finally reached them. "I was hoping to see you here this evening. I meant to call, but I have been fully occupied correcting a mix-up about my rooms here in Bath. My letter reserving them seems to have gone astray."

"How annoying. I hope you have accommodations."

"Now, yes." He turned toward Diana with an expectant smile. He had been too occupied maneuvering through the crowd to look at her before. What he saw struck him dumb with dismay.

"You have met my dear friend Diana Gresham, I believe," said Amanda, a laugh in her voice.

Wilton nodded, swallowing nervously.

Diana, who had observed the change in his expression with surprise and chagrin, merely bowed her head. She had imagined a very different scene when she anticipated this meeting. Why was he so patently disappointed? Was it her face, her gown? Something in her appearance had clearly put him off, and this daunting knowledge made her incapable of speech. She had lost whatever assurance she had once possessed, she saw, in the years of solitude.

"A *very* odd meeting," added Amanda in the silence that followed, puzzlement replacing humor in her tone. "Is it your habit to strike up acquaintance with unknown ladies so, Captain Wilton?"

"No. No." He was too uncomfortable to acknowledge her joke. Robert Wilton had come to this concert solely to meet Diana again. His memory of the girl who had been so sporting about an embarrassing accident had grown rosier with each passing hour. He imagined that he would talk with her as easily as he did with any of his numerous male friends. Her features having been a mystery, he thought of her simply as an attractive personality.

But this hopeful vision had been shattered with his first sight of her gleaming hair, her elegant attire and delicately lovely face. She was even *more* beautiful than the women his mother pushed upon him, and she would no doubt find him as clumsy and tiresome as did they. Wilton cringed mentally at the memory of a succession of excruciating encounters. He knew nothing of London gossip or the current news of close-knit society families, and every girl he had danced with or taken in to dinner in town had made it clear she found him dull and unamusing. His looks were not such as to dazzle, and his long absences from England left his wardrobe outmoded. His wide knowledge of the war and sound views upon it failed to arouse a spark of interest. Thus, he had long ago concluded that he was hopelessly out of place in the drawing room. And now, faced with a Diana no longer covered with mud but resplendent as any society miss, he felt only that he must escape before he saw bored contempt in her eyes too.

Amanda, seeing that, inexplicably, the whole responsibility for conversation rested with her, said, "When did you return to England, Captain Wilton?" Her mystification was plain. Why, she might have been asking, are two people whom I know to be intelligent and interesting standing still and silent as stones?

The implication did nothing to put Wilton at ease. "In July," he replied.

"Just after we did. And have you been staying with your family?"

He nodded quickly and started to make some excuse to take his leave.

"Oh, there is George." Mrs. Trent summoned her husband with a gesture. "George, we have found Robert Wilton."

The two men greeted one another cordially and at once fell into a discussion about Wellington's plans for meeting Napoleon in pitched battle in Flanders.

Diana watched as Captain Wilton's constraint vanished and his blue eyes lit with enthusiasm. He smiled over some remark of George's, and she drew in a breath. She had almost forgotten that smile; it made him seem a different person.

Resentment welled up in her. Why should he be so eager and talkative with George and so sullen and silent with her? What about her offended him? She had done nothing except get in the way of his carriage. But perhaps now that he had seen her, he found she could not compare with the London girls he knew. Diana nodded to herself. Yes, that must be it. He was accustomed to the daughters of the haut ton, and she had none of their polish.

Diana glanced again at Wilton's face, so alive now. That was what he had expected, undoubtedly, and she could not manage it. A sharp pang of disappointment went through her. She had hoped for something from him, she realized, despite her stern resolutions, and she had behaved stupidly, charmed by a man of whom she knew nothing. She must fight this susceptibility in herself, she thought. She would seek an introduction to every gentleman known to the Trents, she decided, and she would treat each of them with equal consideration and interest. That would soon cure her of the lamentable tendency to idealize any one.

And so, as the evening went on, Diana actively encouraged a willing Amanda to present her to officer friends, and she exerted herself mightily to chat and laugh at their sallies. Making conversation was not as difficult as she had feared it might be after her encounter with Robert Wilton. Others appeared flatteringly eager to speak to her, and even reluctant to relinquish places at her side. Diana began to enjoy herself very much indeed, and by the end of the outing had not a glance to spare for Captain Wilton, who stood alone in a corner and watched her with a bitter expression.

5

By the beginning of their fourth day in Bath, Amanda Trent was feeling very pleased indeed with the success of her plans. Diana had been introduced to a great many eligible gentlemen, nearly all soldiers like her own dear husband, and she had made a favorable impression. George himself was far happier, and he was eating better than he had in months. His fellow officers thought nothing of the patch over his eye, for they had seen much worse, and this put him at ease. The opportunity to talk of the war with those whose experience and knowledge matched his own was also important. Indeed, George's spirits were vastly improved; he rarely indulged in fits of melancholy or flashes of temper now. As she tied the strings of her bonnet in preparation for another visit to Milsom Street with Diana, Amanda smiled at her reflection in the mirror.

Diana, in her own bedchamber, was feeling far less content. She had had an unrealistically rosy vision of life in society, she saw. It was not uniformly delightful. The elation she had felt on occasion as she was talking and laughing with a group was offset by moments like the present one, when she was definitely downcast. Living alone, she had experienced neither extreme; each day had been much like the last after her first remorseful months. Now she felt overstimulated and unsure of her reactions, as she had not in years.

Amanda tapped at the door and looked in. "Are you ready?"

"Yes." Diana picked up her gloves and came forward, smiling in a determined effort to convince Amanda that all was well. The Trents had been so kind to her, and it was obvious that Amanda was happy. She would not spoil that.

Passing the drawing room on their way out, they saw Major Trent on the sofa reading a newspaper. "We are going shopping," Amanda told him. "We will be back in time for luncheon if you are staying."

"More new dresses?" answered the major in a joking tone, actually putting aside his paper.

Amanda colored slightly and laughed. "For Diana. She has so few."

George smiled back, reminding Diana for an instant of the young man she had met at their wedding. "Not so much as a ribbon for yourself?"

"Perhaps a ribbon," agreed his wife in the same teasing tone.

"You should get yourself something pretty; you have bought nothing since we came home, I think. Perhaps I will come with you to see that you do."

Amanda drew in her breath and clasped her hands before her. "Really, George?" She turned to Diana. "He has often shopped with me, and found some of my loveliest things. You should see how the shopgirls fawn on him."

This seemed an unfortunate reminiscence, for George's face clouded, making Amanda look as if she wished to bite her tongue. "I should be very glad of your advice," said Diana quickly. "I never had a brother to tell me when I looked truly hideous, and I believe Amanda is rather easy with me."

"I am not!"

"You allowed me to purchase that primrose muslin," retorted Diana, "and when it arrived and I put it on, we both saw that it would not do."

Amanda frowned. "The cloth seemed so different before it was made up. I was sure it would become you."

"You see?" said Diana to George. "Your discriminating opinion is sorely needed." Silently she was wondering how it would be to have a man she scarcely knew help choose her clothes, but she could endure a little embarrassment for Amanda's sake.

"Very well," replied George, rising. He sounded half-eager, half-reluctant.

"Do you remember when we bought that pink silk dress in Lisbon?" asked Amanda. "The dressmaker was scandalized that you came. I'm sure she will always believe Englishmen are mad." She turned to Diana, gratitude for her aid shining in her dark eyes. "She wouldn't even *look* at George. She spoke only to me, as if he weren't there, and if he spoke she answered *me*. It was too ridiculous."

Major Trent laughed. "I don't see why a man shouldn't take an interest in his wife's clothes. I am the one who has to look at them, after all."

"You make it sound such a penance," said Amanda, wrinkling her nose at him.

"Well, when it's a case of black silk with jet beads . . ."

"That wasn't my fault! We lost our way one night in Spain," she informed Diana. "There was a dreadful storm, and we somehow got separated from our escort and luggage. We had to take shelter in a village, the mayor's house. His wife lent me a dress."

"A tent, you mean," said George.

"She *was* rather large."

"Rather? Might as well call Bath 'rather' hilly." The Trents' eyes met, and they laughed together. Diana suddenly understood why Amanda was so fond of him; she felt thrust outside a charmed circle whose warmth and delight had room for only two. "Which brings up the question of transport," added George, breaking the spell. "Do you mean to walk down to town?"

"Oh, yes," said Amanda. "It is not so far, and all downhill." She caught herself. "Would you prefer to ride? Perhaps we should, after all, Diana. I—"

"I am quite up to the walk," interrupted George, and the slip threatened to spoil their new rapprochement.

"The two of you will utterly wear *me* down, I can see," put in Diana. "And I thought I was a redoubtable walker. But let us start out, while I still have the strength."

This elicited another laugh, though less spontaneous than before, and they set out together for the shops. At first, Diana kept up a determined flow of comment on the views from the crescent, the beauty of the Bath streets, and the nature of the crowds they began to encounter lower down. Finally Major Trent put aside his pique, and by the time they reached Milsom Street, they were talking easily together again.

"Here is Madame Riboud's," said Amanda, stopping before an immaculate doorway. "We must go up and see how the rest of Diana's dresses are getting on."

"Why don't you leave me here," suggested Diana. "We could meet in an hour and go on together." She was to have a fitting, and the thought of Major Trent waiting impatiently through it was daunting.

"We might go look at hats," agreed Amanda.

Her husband's face showed that this was a fortunate thought.

"We will come back in an hour to fetch you," she added, "and then we can all go on and buy those artificial flowers you wanted, Diana."

"Ah, I'm just the man to judge *those*," said George. "If you really wish to know what looks hideous . . ."

"Perhaps I don't," laughed Diana, and waved them on their way.

Her new gowns were nearly finished, and she was happy with all of them. Along with her pleasure at George and Amanda's budding reconciliation, this put Diana in a very buoyant mood, and when she descended the stairs from Madame Riboud's a little more than an hour later to find no one awaiting her, she did not care a whit. Bath was a very safe town, she knew, and the Trents would no doubt appear soon.

She gazed at the goods offered in nearby shop windows, strolling a little way along the pavement and then back in the opposite direction. Should she go in search of them? she wondered, but concluded that they would only miss one another.

Peering up and down the street again, hoping to see her friends, she abruptly encountered the hugely magnified eye of a man across the way, who was examining her through a kind of glass on a gilded stick. His appearance was so astonishing that she did not immediately turn away. Diana had never seen anyone in pale lavender pantaloons, a primrose coat so tight she could not imagine how its wearer got it on, a blinding brocade waistcoat, and a neckcloth so high and starched and intricate she wondered if it were linen or carved of wood and painted. Simultaneously raising one pale eyebrow and one corner of his mouth, the man sauntered toward her, his quizzing glass now dangling negligently from his white hand.

"How d'ye do?" he said when he had picked his way delicately across the cobbles. "Lost your way?"

"Why, no." Diana was too fascinated by his grotesque appearance to snub him. And she had never learned to administer a setdown in any case.

"Couldn't help noticin' you wanderin' about the street." The man smirked. He had a drawling, lisping way of speaking that Diana found as bizarre as his apparel.

"I'm waiting for my friends," she replied, her voice cool.

"Ah. Beg pardon for intrudin'." He looked her over with a connoisseur's eye. "Ronald Boynton," he added hopefully.

This was too much. Diana did not give her name to total strangers in the street. Robert Wilton had been a definite exception. And she found Boynton ridiculous. She merely inclined her head and pointedly searched again for the Trents.

He took her lead without protest. "Must be goin'. Perhaps we'll meet in the Pump Room? Visitin' my aunt here, you know. Deuced flat, but . . ." He shrugged elaborately and, when she did not reply, bowed, sweeping the pavement with the brim of his hat, and turned away. Diana watched him go. He minced, she thought with an incredulous smile; one couldn't call it anything else.

"Whoever was *that?*" said Amanda Trent behind her, and Diana swung around. They had come up when she was looking the other way.

"A Mr. Ronald Boynton," she answered, still smiling. "He thought I was lost."

"He accosted you in the street! Oh, Diana, I am so

sorry we are late. We lost track of the time, and . . ."

"It doesn't matter, Amanda. He wasn't the least offensive. Just . . . odd. Have you ever seen such an outfit!"

"Often," said her friend, her worried expression easing. "That, Diana, is a dandy."

George muttered.

"Indeed?" Diana looked again, but Mr. Boynton was gone. "Is that what they look like? Amazing."

"You were taken with him, I see." Amanda grinned mischievously.

"Oh, of course." She essayed an imitation of Boynton's speech. "He was so very charmin', you know."

Amanda burst out laughing, and George, who had begun to glower, saw the joke and smiled slightly. "Well, he must have been taken with you," Amanda crowed. "I daresay he will dog your footsteps."

"He had better not," exclaimed her husband.

"I don't suppose we shall ever see him again," replied Diana. "Did you buy a hat?"

Diverted, the Trents launched into an antiphonal description of their shopping expedition, which had clearly been both successful and enjoyable. Diana watched their happy faces, Boynton forgotten, recovering her pleasant mood in their pleasure.

They visited one or two more shops before returning home in great charity with one another to a cold luncheon. Diana could not recall a jollier occasion with the Trents, or perhaps with anyone. Her despondency of the morning had been silly, she told herself. It would simply take her a little time to become accustomed to a new way of living.

"Diana," said Amanda, in a tone that implied it was not the first time she had spoken.

"What?"

"You were far away. I merely asked if you are looking forward to your first assembly ball this evening."

"Oh. Yes."

"I admit I am, too. How long is it since we danced, George?"

"Before I was wounded," he answered curtly, but his tone was not as bitter as it had once been.

"So it was. You will stand up with me tonight, will you not? We met at just such an occasion, remember?"

He nodded slowly, turning to watch her face. After a moment, he put a hand over hers on the table, and Amanda smiled up at him.

"I must see about my dress," said Diana, rising. The Trents would not always want her about, she thought. She must be careful not to intrude on their first real respite after years abroad. Neither answered, and as she left the room Diana felt a novel wistfulness. It must be wonderful to have a close companion who shared one's interests and confidences, she thought. This was a side to love she had not observed before, and for that reason it seemed more attractive than the violent ups and downs of her youth. Was such a closeness possible for her even yet? she wondered. The idea was so thrilling, and at the same time so improbable, that she thrust it from her mind and turned resolutely to the question of a ball gown.

In this at least, her choice was easy. Her first ball dress had been waiting for her at the dressmaker's that morning. Diana had instructed her to finish it before the others, for she had no suitable garment for the Bath assemblies, and she was more than pleased with the results. Made of a bronze satin just the shade of her hair and trimmed with knots of silver ribbon, Diana's dress was stunning. When Amanda had suggested the combination, Diana had at first been doubtful, but she was now very glad that she had allowed herself to be persuaded. The gown was striking and distinctive, the two burnished colors a happy change from the usual white or pink, and not at all garish. As Amanda had promised, the dress accentuated Diana's unique look, and Diana anticipated wearing it with a thrill of pleasure.

George and Amanda concurred when they all met in the hall before leaving. Amanda could not stop exclaiming at how well the gown had turned out, and with a smile George complimented Diana on her appearance. His mellow mood had lasted through the day.

"Oh, isn't this splendid?" said Amanda as they ate. "A true assembly. And Diana is going to make such a hit."

"I shall be satisfied if I am not left standing too often during the dancing," laughed Diana. "Do not set your hopes too high."

"Nonsense. You will be mobbed; wait and see."

Diana merely shook her head.

The assembly rooms were very near their lodgings, and they decided to walk, as the night was fine. They had left their wraps and were moving through the octagon room toward the main ballroom when Major Trent was stopped by a group of friends. As they paused to allow him to exchange greetings, Diana looked around the anteroom. Men and women in evening dress stood about, flirting and laughing. The dresses surpassed any Diana had seen before this visit. Strains of music could be heard above the buzz of talk, and the air was heady with the scents of perfumes and pomades. Her heart began to beat a little faster, and she drew in her breath. One of the Trents' friends whom she had met caught her eye and came forward to request a dance. Diana looked to Amanda, received a smiling dismissal, and went off on his arm.

The first part of the evening was even better than Diana had expected. Due to the Trents' wide acquaintance and her own attractions, she was never without a partner, and her hasty practice the night before had brought suitable proficiency in the various steps. She went in to supper with a very charming young lieutenant and a party of his friends, and then she danced the first set after the interval with a dashing cavalry officer. The gentlemen seemed to judge her conversation engrossing, another hurdle that had worried her after years alone, and all in all, Diana felt her first assembly ball a great success until she spied Robert Wilton lounging aganst the far wall near the end of the cotillion.

His arms were crossed on his chest, and he watched the dancers with a curled lip. He thinks us all contemptible, Diana thought. Though the thought made her angry—for what right had he to sneer?—she was also conscious of a sharp disappointment. She had been hoping to see him, she realized, and perhaps even to dance with him, wiping out the memory of their last awkward encounter. But now this seemed most unlikely. Wilton turned his head, and their eyes met, then dropped immediately. Diana, cursing her clumsiness, raised hers again at once, but he was no longer looking in her direction. Her poise left her where Mr. Wilton was concerned. Her years of solitude had left their mark to this degree. Diana bit her lower lip in vexation and returned her attention to her partner.

Captain Wilton clenched his jaw and stared at the floor rather than the whirling couples. Why had he come here? he was asking himself. It was just the sort of occasion he most hated and was most likely to bring off poorly. His mother could not drag him to a ball in London, and yet he had rigged himself out and appeared here with no urging, only to be as miserable as he would have been there. He had *not* come because of a girl with bronze hair and gold-flecked eyes; yet his gaze strayed toward Diana again.

"Hello, Captain Wilton," said Amanda Trent. She was floating by on her husband's arm, nearly bursting with happiness because the evening was going so well. The gentlemen acknowledged each other cordially as the music ended. "Are you enjoying the assembly?" added Amanda, in a tone which suggested that everyone must be as pleased as she.

He shrugged, not wishing to appear surly, but unable to give the expected reply.

Amanda noticed his unease fleetingly—she was too engrossed in her own far different feelings to linger over his—and with some surprise. But as Diana's partner just then delivered her back to her party, Amanda had an inspiration. "Diana, here is your old acquaintance Captain Wilton. You must not refuse him a dance."

Diana, startled, replied that she had no such intention, and raised surprised, but not displeased, eyes to his face.

Wilton, taken unawares, allowed his chagrin to show.

"Oh, it is a waltz, too," continued Amanda blithely. "George, we must dance. And, Diana, you needn't hesitate. There are no fusty Almack's patronesses in Bath." The Trents joined the dancers.

The captain hung back.

Diana flushed. "You needn't dance with me if you don't wish to," she said bluntly. "I shall be quite all right alone here." Diana's chin was high. "I daresay someone else may even ask me. You needn't feel *obliged.*" His response to Amanda's ploy had hurt her, and she didn't care if she made him feel boorish.

"I beg your pardon," he answered stiffly. "I cannot yet dance." With a gesture, he indicated the ebony cane leaning beside him.

Overcome with mortification, Diana blushed a deeper crimson. She had forgotten all about his wound. She had been thinking only of herself, and had behaved heedlessly and callously. "I . . . I'm sorry," she stammered. "I—"

"It doesn't signify," he interrupted, but his tone belied his words. Clearly, he felt his inability irksome. He stood very straight and gazed out over her head at the ballroom.

She must do something to make amends, Diana thought. "Would you . . . that is, we could sit down and talk, if you like," she stammered, feeling awkward.

Wilton looked down, surprised. He had expected her to go in search of a partner who could dance. "I'm no good at pretty speeches and fulsome compliments," he said, and waited for the inevitable withdrawal.

But Diana's reaction was immediate sympathy and understanding. She knew only too well what it was to feel out of place. Could this assured-looking man really experience some of the same embarrassments? "No, only at covering people with mud," she replied, with a smile to show that she was rallying him.

He stared, then laughed. "Indeed. And like most of my skills, scarcely sought after in society."

"But you *can* sit? When you wish to?" Diana's dark eyes sparkled up at him.

He was amazed and delighted. He had never met such a girl in London. "I can."

"And . . . ?"

Wilton frowned in puzzlement.

"*Do* you wish to?" If he said no, Diana thought, she would never attempt such a joking exchange again.

But his smile reappeared. "I do indeed." They moved together to two gilt chairs against the wall and sat side by side.

"I must say I wonder why you came," said Diana.

Once again Captain Wilton found himself at a loss, but the feeling was far different from that he customarily experienced in London. Diana Gresham was not bored with him or contemptuous of his dress and manners, nor did her eyes wander to more fashionable gentlemen nearby. Her attention was squarely on him, though its focus was wholly unexpected. Drawing on a nimble wit and flexibility that had gotten him out of some of the nastiest spots in the Penninsula, Wilton set himself to match her. "I suppose I can't give up the habit of reconnoitering when in hostile territory."

Pleased in her turn, Diana thought about this. "Would you call us hostile?"

"Not so much as in London, perhaps."

The corners of her mouth turned up. "Where you received your training?"

He nodded feelingly.

"Some would envy you such a school. It is, after all, the center for these arts."

"And it may keep them!"

Seeing that he really felt strongly on this subject, Diana modulated her tone. "You really do not enjoy—?" she began.

"No, I cannot. Put me on a battlefield, or carrying a message fifty miles across Spain, and I am content. I should far rather face the French batteries than a line of simpering chits at Almack's. There are a thousand more important questions in life than the Duchess of Rutland's rout party or Prinny's new mistress." He flushed. "I beg your pardon. I should not have mentioned—"

"Of course there are," she agreed, ignoring his slip. "But must one worry over them all the time? Do you grudge a moment's frivolity?"

"In times such as these, this"—he indicated the room with a glance—"is a waste of time and irritation to any true Englishman."

"Thank you, sir," Diana could not help replying, though she was not really angry. His vehemence was irresistible.

For a moment he did not understand her. Then he grimaced. "I did not mean you."

"I know what you meant. You are right, I'm sure. It is just that I know so little about the war. And I admit I am enjoying my first taste of gaiety, despite it."

"First?" he asked, intrigued, for she was not a child fresh from the schoolroom.

Immediately Diana wished she had held her tongue. "I . . . I have lived at home until now."

"Far from Bath?"

"Yes, in Yorkshire." And now he would inquire why she had not been to the York assemblies, or to London, Diana thought wearily, and she would have no satisfactory answer, and he would believe that she was administering a setdown when she turned his questions aside.

But Robert Wilton had heard the reluctance in her voice, and no one knew better than he the agonies of awkward inquiries. Without seeking reasons, he shifted the subject. "You are fortunate. The Bath assemblies are much jollier than those in London."

Diana gazed at him with relief and amazement, and met blue eyes that communicated an acknowledgment of her constraint, and of her right to avoid its source if she chose. She had to swallow a sudden lump in her throat. "But less brilliant," she managed to respond.

Wilton shrugged as if to say this was a matter of definition.

Surprising both of them, the music ended. The set had seemed very short. They drew apart—for they had been leaning rather markedly toward one another, they discovered—and looked around for the Trents.

Amanda and George were on the far side of the room. Wilton reached for his ebony cane. "Don't get up," said Diana.

"I am perfectly able to walk," he replied, with some impatience but none of the bitterness she had heard in George Trent. "My knee is only a bit stiff. The doctors say I shall be completely restored in a month or so."

"Does it pain you?" asked Diana hesitantly as they started across the room.

"Very little. And it requires exercise." He smiled down at her. "So you see, you are doing me a good turn."

Once again Diana was struck by the force of his smile. "Perhaps I should insist upon a turn about the room."

"Perhaps you should."

Their eyes held for a long moment, and each felt that there was some special quality in this new acquaintance that demanded further exploration.

"Wilton!" exclaimed a drawling voice behind them.

"No idea you were in Bath, old man. How d'ye do?"

They turned to confront a vision in fawn pantaloons and a dark blue coat hung with a profusion of fobs and so starched and cinched and padded that he could scarcely move. Diana, astounded, looked from Captain Wilton to Ronald Boynton and back again. Was it possible that these two were acquainted?

"Left Faring in fine form," continued Boynton. "Took a hand with him at White's just before I left town. His usual damnable luck." He stopped, turned to Diana, and shook his head. "Beg pardon. No wish to offend. Feelings got the better of me." He then gave Wilton such a speaking look that the latter was forced to make introductions, though he was obviously reluctant to do so.

Diana, as she acknowledged him, wondered if Boynton would refer to their earlier encounter. But he merely raised one pale eyebrow meaningfully and went on talking of himself.

"Toddled up to visit my Aunt Miranda, you know. Ill. No good neglectin' the family fortune."

"Is your aunt very wealthy?" inquired Diana, unable to resist. She glanced at the captain, to share her amusement with him, but he was scowling at the floor.

"Rich as Golden Ball," replied Boynton promptly. "Refuses to make a final will, too. Have to keep in her good books." He smiled ingratiatingly. "Care to dance?"

Diana hesitated only a moment. Wilton had been about to leave her in any case, and her sense of the ridiculous was aroused. Also, she realized suddenly, Boynton reminded her of her long-ago love Gerald Carshin. It was not that the two men were really alike, she thought, it was merely the style of dress and something in Boynton's manner which piqued her curiosity. How would she respond to such a man now, when she felt so much changed? Her initial reaction suggested that she had in fact matured in ways that pleased her, but she was not averse to a further test. She agreed.

Wilton, watching her go off on the dandy's arm, felt a surge of fury. That the woman he had found it possible to talk with so easily, and had begun to admire, should so blithely accept Boynton reignited all his former doubts. Wilton thoroughly despised his brother Faring's set; they were lazy, affected, and disgracefully unmoved by the important issues of the day. They cared for nothing but gaming, gossip, and . . . Here he paused in horror, recalling some of his brother's more unsavory romantic entanglements.

Miss Gresham could have no idea of the sort of man she had consented to partner. An innocent such as she, never having gone into society, would not know how to take his extravagant compliments and false praise. She must be warned, he thought. Yet what right had he to be concerned about such things? She had friends in Bath. But looking over his shoulder at the Trents merely reaffirmed his fears. They knew almost as little as Diana of the "smart set." He would have to do something. With this determination, he returned to his chair, wholly unaware that his charitable impulse had its roots in a fierce jealousy. Had anyone inquired, he would have staunchly maintained that he felt only concern for Miss Gresham's welfare, and perhaps a mild disappointment that she should be taken in by such a contemptible specimen.

The captain would have been astonished could he have known with what amused disbelief Diana listened to her elegant companion. He was very like Gerald, she was concluding. Gerald had said just the same sort of things to her, and gazed at her in the same soulful way. How incredibly silly she had been at seventeen, to have been taken in by this nonsense. Yet this demonstration of past mistakes also reassured her. Certainly she had learned her lesson. She was not the naive, impressionable child who had gotten into such a scrape. This also meant, she concluded happily, that her judgment was now trustworthy. She need not be worried if she found recent acquaintances very attractive. Smiling, she looked around the ballroom. Captain Wilton had taken up his station against the wall once more, arms crossed. How mulish he looked.

Diana laughed for sheer joy, causing her partner to smirk complacently, sure that he had made a conquest, and making a certain young soldier not far away grit his teeth so violently his jaw ached.

6

Diana and Amanda were alone at the breakfast table the following morning. George had gone out for an early ride, as the April day was unusually fine, and the two women took advantage of their solitude to indulge in a thorough discussion of the assembly. When they had reviewed the recent history of all the Trents' old friends, the particularly striking toilettes each had noticed, and the pleasure each had felt in dancing, Amanda fixed her friend with twinkling eyes. "Now, Diana, you must say which of your partners you liked best. That is the obligation of an unmarried girl, and the prerogative of a married woman is to interrogate."

"You are scarcely two years older than I," she laughed.

"Do not try to divert me. Which?"

The gold flecks in Diana's eyes sparkled. "Mr. Boynton asked me to stand up with him. Did you see?"

"Boynton! You cannot mean that ridiculous man who accosted you in the street! Did he actually force himself upon you? Diana, you should have—"

"No, no. I was properly introduced. Captain Wilton presented me."

Amanda's mouth dropped open, and her dark eyes grew round.

Diana could not help but laugh again. "It seems Mr. Boynton is a friend of his brother's."

"Ah. That explains it. I daresay Captain Wilton was not overpleased to meet him here."

"No, I don't think he was."

"I was so mortified when I realized that I had placed Robert in an awkward position. I should have realized that he cannot dance yet. I hope he was not offended."

Diana shook her head.

"And you are not telling me that Mr. Boynton was your favorite partner, Diana."

"Why not?" But she smiled.

Amanda did not even acknowledge this. "No. But perhaps . . . Robert Wilton?" She raised her eyebrows.

"I like him," admitted Diana, never having been schooled in dissimulation.

"He is a fine fellow. Yet not so handsome as Major Beresford. Or so polished as Colonel Ellmann. If it weren't for George, I should develop a tendre for him myself." She watched Diana closely as she spoke these names, and gathered more information than Diana dreamed from her expression.

"They are charming," she agreed. "But what of you, Amanda? You enjoyed the ball?"

"You are trying to turn the subject!"

"I?" Diana was all mock astonishment.

Her friend laughed and let it go. She had found out what she wanted to know in any case. "I had a splendid time."

"George seemed to enjoy himself, too."

"Yes." This word was spoken softly and gratefully. "Oh, Diana, I truly believe he is getting over his melancholy, and his weakness. This visit was an inspiration. Things are so much better between us."

"I am glad," Diana replied, sincerely, but with some reticence. She did not know how to treat confidences about marital difficulties. She wished to lend her aid without prying, and this line seemed fine.

Amanda appeared to understand. "What shall we do today?" she asked with a warm smile. "More shopping?"

"Not yet. I have had enough of dressmakers and milliners for a while. I have begun to feel like some sort of doll, pinned and prodded and spoken of as if I were not present, or perhaps merely half-witted."

"What then?" laughed her friend.

"A walk? Or perhaps a drive in the countryside?" Diana had been feeling the need for space and air. She was accustomed to daily tramps on the moors in all weathers. "You needn't come if you don't wish to."

"I should like a drive. I have never seen the country about here. Shall we go this afternoon? George may come with us."

Diana nodded. "Perhaps you would prefer to go together. You needn't feel that I—"

"You are the soul of discretion," interrupted Amanda, and they exchanged a look which said all that was necessary on this subject. Diana was relieved to see that she had not been a burden. "I shall write some letters this morning, then," she went on.

"I will begin my new novel."

The two ladies thus settled happily in the drawing room after breakfast, and for some time the comfortable silence was broken only by the scratching of Amanda's pen and the rustle of pages as Diana turned them. Occasionally, looking up from her novel, the latter felt a marvelous contentment. She had never imagined, living in isolation these past years, that she would come to this.

Around midmorning the bell rang, and the maid came up to announce a caller. Amanda gave her friend a speaking glance as Captain Robert Wilton was announced, and gave orders that he should be admitted at once. Diana closed her book, started to rise, then simply sat straighter in her chair.

Wilton appeared, leaning slightly on his cane, and greeted them both.

"George should be back at any moment," said Amanda. "Do sit down." She moved from the writing desk to the sofa.

He hesitated, then joined her, taking the end nearest Diana's chair. There was a short silence.

"A fine day," said Amanda. The others agreed. "I hope you enjoyed the assembly last night, Captain Wilton?"

"As much as one can, in these days. I am not one of those who can enjoy fripperies while important events are afoot abroad." He had meant this to open the way to a discreet warning about Boynton. All night, he had been absorbed with the necessity to guard Diana, and he had called with this single desire. But as soon as he spoke, and took in their response, he saw that he had blundered. "I did not mean that you . . ." he began. "That is, I was referring to those who never consider serious matters. An evening's entertainment is certainly harmless, but there are those . . ." He ran down, miserably aware of his lack of finesse.

"Of course," agreed Amanda, wondering a little what her friend so admired in this man. He was well enough, but she herself was drawn to rather a different type. With a smile, she remembered a younger George and the way he had swept into her life.

"I understood that the regimental officers grasped every opportunity to arrange amusements during the pauses in the fighting," said Diana, both to end the constrained silence and to make a point. It was all very well to complain that those at home ignored the war and she understood his feelings, but it was not universally true, and she thought Captain Wilton a little single-minded. Diana had heard a great deal about soldiers' lighter moments last night. "Not only dancing, but racing and all manner of other things."

"Oh, yes," said Amanda. "Wellington loves balls. And I remember once a young lieutenant in George's regiment organized a donkey race. The riders had to sit backward. It was the funniest thing I ever saw." She grinned impishly. "George won. You must ask him about it."

Diana had seen Captain Wilton's lips twitch. "But you did nothing so frivolous, I suppose," she said.

"Compensation for hardship is somewhat different," he responded, a reminiscent gleam in his blue eyes.

"Indeed, I have suddenly remembered," put in Amanda. "Were you not one of those responsible for the 'fox' hunt before Vitoria?" She turned to Diana, her eyes dancing again. "They flushed a weasel, and pursued it six miles."

Wilton burst out laughing. "Pluck up to the backbone, that weasel. Led us a merry dance, and got away in the end. Of course, our pack wasn't quite up to snuff."

"Three young hounds, a poodle, and a cocker spaniel," giggled Amanda. Diana laughed with them, happy for the turn the conversation had taken.

"The poodle had some natural talent," the captain informed her seriously, "but the cocker kept losing her nerve and turning for home. Our master of the hounds had a dev . . . deuced time keeping them to the scent."

"Of the *weasel,*" added Amanda.

"Exactly."

His smile made his eyes crinkle at the outer corners, Diana thought, and they held an entrancing mixture of warm humor, mischievousness, and generosity.

Meeting Diana's interested gaze, he added, "I do not mean that everyone should be gloomy and think of nothing but the progress of the fighting. Far from it. But those who pretend that Napoleon does not exist, or that the war is simply a great spectacle put on for their entertainment, rouse my fury. Like your friend Boynton. He has a dubious reputation, you know."

Amanda's dark eyes lit with amusement, seeing why the captain had come. Diana was merely surprised. She opened her mouth to say that he was no friend of hers, just as the maid announced, "Mr. Ronald Boynton, ma'am."

Amanda had to bite her lower lip as she rose to greet the new arrival. It was too ridiculous, she thought, that the man should come in at just the instant to cause such chagrin, of different sorts, in her two companions. It was almost like a play.

Mr. Boynton rose from bowing over her hand, and turned to favor Diana with the same attention. "Miss Gresham," he murmured. "Lovelier than ever."

Captain Wilton returned his cordial nod with a glower, but this did not seem to strike Boynton as unusual. "I called to see how you did after the fatigues of the assembly," he added as he sat down.

"It ended at eleven," Diana pointed out. Bath hours were not London's.

Boynton acknowledged the difference with a grimace. "Indeed. I was speakin' of the fatigue engendered by tedium. I have never in my life encountered such a set of dowds and bores. I declare, some old pokerface bent my ear for more than an hour about some rubbishin' sea battle. Can you credit it?"

"Admiral Riley perhaps," answered Wilton, his voice filled with contempt.

"I shouldn't be surprised. I don't know why I come to Bath. It's always so."

"Well, why not go home, then," said Amanda, polite but hardly warm.

Boynton grinned, leaning back in his chair and twirling his quizzing glass in one negligent hand. "Must dance attendance on my aunt, actually. Holds the purse strings. Been dippin' a trifle deep at White's, too." He looked around as if to gather their admiration for this fashionable admission. "A spell of rustication was called for."

With a small smile, Diana wondered what he would think of her home if he called Bath rustication. She imagined Mr. Boynton forced to spend even a month in her lonely house, and her smile widened.

Captain Wilton saw her expression with annoyance. How could she be amused by this lisping coxcomb? No sensible woman would endure him for a moment. Oddly, it did not occur to the captain that he and his mother and sisters had often found his brother Faring and his friends hilarious, and that they often rallied him unmercifully about his dandiacal dress and mannerisms. Diana's response seemed something quite different, and ominous.

"Are you drinking the waters?" asked Amanda, angling for further amusement.

Boynton looked horrified. "I? No, no. Leave that to my aunt."

"She is ill?"

"So she says. For my part, I think she enjoys playin' the invalid and keepin' her family dancin' attendance round her bedside. Not a bad life, lyin' about, eatin' chocolates and readin' novels, and gettin' up whenever there is anything interestin' on."

"You are speaking of Lady Overton?" asked Wilton. Diana was struck by the change in his voice. Before, he had sounded so accessible and charming; now his tone might have frozen the most impervious intruder.

Boynton, however, did not seem to notice. He nodded. "That's it."

"I understood that she has been seriously ill all year. My mother mentioned that she nearly died recently."

The other man shrugged. "So she says. Myself, I think it's just another excuse to change her will." He turned to Diana. "She alters the deuced thing every month. One never knows where one is."

Wilton threw Diana a speaking look, as if to say: You see how callous and selfish this man is. Diana, who had reached a similar conclusion long ago, merely smiled slightly at him and lowered her eyes.

"So how is the knee?" Boynton added. "Faring mentioned you'd been hit. How long will your leave last? Perhaps you can muster out?"

"I shall return to my regiment as soon as the last stiffness goes." Wilton's face was like stone.

Boynton shook his head. "You military fellows. Fire-breathers, eh? Can't see it myself." He turned to Diana. "I mean, the regimentals are all very well. Dashin', some of them. But you're bound to be posted abroad, and then where are you?"

"Just now, Belgium," snapped Wilton, goaded.

"Exactly." Boynton beamed on them all as if he had scored a hit.

Captain Wilton started to rise. He had had enough. "I must go," he began, only to be interrupted by the entrance of George Trent.

"Some damn fool has left a high-perch phaeton in our stableyard," he said without preamble. "I could hardly get Thunderer past to the door." He surveyed the unwelcome crowd in his drawing room, looking quite daunting with his black eyepatch and impatient expression.

"Oh, dear," answered Amanda. "I wonder whose . . . ?"

"It's mine," said Boynton. "Bought it only three weeks ago, and couldn't resist bringin' it along to Bath. Slap up to the echo, what?" Belatedly, under George's furious gaze, he added, "Sorry if it was blockin' you. Stupid groom ought to have moved."

"Who," growled Trent, "are you?"

At once Boynton was on his feet and bowing. "Beg your pardon. Forgot we hadn't been introduced. Ronald Boynton. Friend of Miss Gresham's, you know."

This shifted George's outraged attention to Diana, who nearly gasped at the unfairness of it. Friend, indeed!

Amanda made a gurgling noise, and Robert Wilton could not restrain a smile. Diana's face had been so transparently readable.

"A new acquaintance, rather," Diana said.

Boynton bowed again. "Alas. But with great hopes."

"Fribble!" exploded George.

Everyone was still for a moment. Wilton was obviously struggling with a strong urge to laugh. Amanda looked amused but concerned at his rudeness. Diana was merely taken aback, and Boynton did not believe his ears. "Beg pardon?" he replied finally.

"Idiotic sort of carriage anyway," added George.

"Impractical, and deuced dangerous. Wouldn't have one on a wager."

Boynton's shock deepened. "But my dear sir. Phaeton. Absolutely all the crack, y'know. Why, Prinny himself—"

"Bonehead," muttered George, much more quietly than before. He was recovering his manners, slowly.

"Prinny!" exclaimed Boynton, aghast. "You really mustn't say such things. Not aloud, at least. No, really, he's dashed sensitive. Why, ever since Brummell remarked on his—"

"I'll say what I like in my own house!" roared Major Trent. "And I was speaking of you, you jingling fop."

Ronald Boynton was for a rare instant struck completely dumb. He did not entirely object to the epithet "fop," but the tone of the major's voice had made his contempt obvious, and Boynton was so accustomed to thinking of himself as the height of fashion—absolutely top of the trees—that it took him a moment to assimilate. When he had, he first gaped at the man, then shook his head. Clearly his host was as crude and ignorant as he looked. Years in benighted outposts far from London had blighted him beyond rescue. Boynton felt sincere pity for the ladies forced to live with such a barbarian. He threw them a commiserating glance. "Perhaps I should take my leave," he suggested gently.

"Splendid idea," replied Trent.

Boynton made a moue at Diana, shrugged slightly to show Amanda that he fully understood her plight, and made his way out of the room.

"Coxcomb," said George, dropping into a chair. "Why did you let him in, Amanda?"

"Susan brought him up without asking. We did have

another caller, after all." She indicated Wilton with a nod.

"Yes. Hallo, Wilton. Well, you must tell the girl not to admit him after this. I can't stand the creature. Diana, you should not be making such friends."

This was too much. Diana hadn't a particle of interest in Boynton, beyond mild amusement, but to be continually taxed with his friendship and blamed for his faults, and then forbidden something she had never desired, annoyed her into answering, "He is perfectly harmless, after all. I do not see what all the fuss is about."

"I shouldn't be too sure of that," said Wilton.

"Oh, you are all just as bad as the Londoners!" Diana stood. "They close their minds to the war, but you think of nothing else. Must everyone be so earnest and solemn that he cannot even laugh at the affectations of a man like Boynton? *I* shall not become so!" And with this, she gathered her skirts and swept out of the room. Robert Wilton's censorious looks were simply beyond bearing. Why could he not be as before? Why must their growing understanding be spoiled by this idiocy?

In the drawing room, the three remaining exchanged an uneasy glance.

"I didn't mean . . ." began George.

"I was only trying . . ." said Wilton at the same time.

"Never mind," replied Amanda. "She will be all right in a bit."

7

A HALF-HOUR LATER, WHEN WILTON HAD GONE AND George was immersed in the newspaper, Amanda went upstairs to find Diana. When her knock had been acknowledged, she put her head around the door of Diana's bedchamber and said, "Are you all right?"

Diana sat in an armchair next to the window, chin in hand, looking out. "Yes, of course. I'm sorry I lost my temper. It was silly."

Amanda came in. "No, it wasn't. Why *should* you think of nothing but the war? You were quite right; one must have a balance. You see, George and his friends have done nothing but fight for so long—many of them since they were little more than boys, actually—that it is difficult for them to shift their thoughts. And it is particularly hard for them now, since the outcome of this war is about to be decided all over again, and they are not allowed to be there. And when it is a question of gossip or assemblies, which would not interest George, at least, even in the calmest times . . . well . . ." She shrugged.

Diana grimaced. "I know. I was stupid. It was just that they seemed to hold me responsible for Boynton's presence, and"—she spread her hands, searching for a phrase strong enough and failing to find one—"I am *not.*"

"Of course you are not." Amanda smiled. "They

know that. They were simply making pronouncements, as men will do. They are almost always sorry afterward."

"What do you mean?"

Amanda colored slightly. "Well, it is a thing I have noticed. Men are fond of sweeping statements, don't you think? They like to tie everything up in a phrase which is often quite outrageously untrue, and rush on. Later, when they are cooler, they will be reasonable." She hesitated, considering. "Actually, they usually forget the matter entirely, and you can quietly do as you like. I remember we had a cook once . . ." She paused. "But you don't care for that."

"On the contrary," answered Diana. "I am fascinated." She was also impressed, as she had been several times before, with the changes in Amanda since they had known one another as girls. Diana had had no opportunity to observe the male sex or learn its quirks. Amanda had, and Diana sensed that her friend had made the most of her chance. "Do you not sometimes feel deceitful?" she asked.

"When I do as I please despite George's commands?" Amanda pondered this. "But he doesn't really *mean* it, you see. That is, sometimes he does, and I can tell. In *those* cases, I either obey or tell him my opinion, and we discuss the matter." She smiled. " 'Discuss' is a mild word for some of those occasions. But mostly he just needs to explode; often it is about something quite different from our conversation—an orderly's stupidity perhaps, or poor forage for his men. Afterward he is all right again. He does not *really* care where I purchase my chickens or"—she smiled at Diana—"whether I enjoy a ball and forget about the war. He is merely . . . fulminating."

Diana laughed. "What a word."

Her friend's eyes danced. "I learned it from a lieutenant of artillery."

"But do you really think that they will forget all about Boynton and all of that"—she made a helpless gesture—"this morning?"

"Oh, George will. He will scarcely remember Mr. Boynton's existence tomorrow." She dimpled. "Unless he should happen to leave his phaeton in George's path again, and I doubt he will."

Diana frowned, taking this in.

"With Captain Wilton, the case is rather different, I think," Amanda added slowly, watching her face.

"Why?"

"Well, I'm not certain, mind, but I believe that he was jealous."

"Jealous?" Diana was incredulous. "Of Mr. Boynton? But what reason could he possibly have . . . ?"

"Boynton is very elegant. Many women are dazzled by such as he. And he *does* seem to be taken with you."

"But do you mean Captain Wilton would be bothered because I danced with Mr. Boynton? Do you think he would care . . . ?" Diana broke off, confused and thrilled by this new idea. The possibility that Robert Wilton resented her acknowledgment of another man, even such a pallid one as she had given Boynton, was not unpleasing. Indeed, the thought made her smile slightly and gaze out the window from under lowered eyelids. Seen in this light, the morning's events looked quite different. Her resentment toward Wilton dissolved, though she still believed she had been right to speak as she had.

Amanda had no trouble interpreting her look. "Why do you like him so?" she asked. "I mean, he is well enough, but . . . I don't mean to offend you."

Diana shook her head. "It is the way he *is*. That is a

poor explanation, I know, but I am not certain I can better it. He is . . . oh, aware of one's hesitations and willing to let them be. He understands that others may feel what he does not, and just as deeply. He is intelligent and amusing." Diana shrugged. "And of course he has the most wonderful smile. I think him handsome."

"I never said he wasn't," began Amanda, then paused as she saw the other's teasing look. She shook her head. "Incorrigible. Your reasons are very sound; I am impressed. I was not half so sensible when I first met George."

This made Diana look up quickly, then down. Amanda was not mocking her, but the comparison somehow saddened Diana and dissipated the warm glow she had been feeling. She was being sensible, just as she had been so entirely the opposite seven years ago. Yet "sensible," when spoken aloud, sounded so drearily practical and dull. In a sudden flash, she remembered her trembling excitement when she had gone to meet Gerald Carshin as a girl. Had it gone forever? Yet it had brought her ony disaster. Raising her chin, Diana took herself firmly in hand. She was wiser as well as older now, and she would be guided by her "sensible" mind.

In the afternoon, postponing their drive, Amanda and Diana walked down into the town to visit the Pump Room. It was not the fashionable hour, but Amanda had been feeling a trifle unwell the past few days, and she had decided to try the waters. They kept a leisurely pace, gazing into shop windows and stopping once to speak to an acquaintance. When they reached the rooms, they found them sparsely populated. Amanda went at once to the gleaming pumps and procured a glass, drawn for her by one of the attendants. "It smells nasty," she said when it had been handed her, sniffing doubtfully at the contents.

"Throw it away," suggested Diana, who wholeheartedly agreed.

"Oh, no. They were so kind in getting it, and they would see."

"We can walk into another room."

Amanda shook her head. "I mean to drink it. I haven't been feeling the thing at all. It is just . . ." She eyed the glass.

Diana laughed. "Well, you decide. I would chuck it out the window. But I will support you while you drink. Shall we sit down?"

They did, and Amanda took a small sip. "Ugh."

Diana couldn't help but laugh again, though she pressed her lips together when Amanda shot her an indignant look.

"It is all very well for you. You never complain of so much as a headache. I suppose you have no idea how uncomfortable it is to feel your whole insides heaving about like the sea."

"I fear not." Diana's eyes sparkled.

Amanda took another tiny sip. "Well, perhaps I shall slip something into your dinner one night, to show you. It is the most dreadful sensation."

"I'm sure it must be," replied her friend, truly sympathetic.

"Oh, look, there is Mr. Boynton. Do you suppose that is his aunt?"

Diana turned to see Ronald Boynton escorting a very large older woman into the Pump Room. They moved slowly, less, it appeared, because of the lady's vast bulk than due to her health. It was obvious that she had been seriously ill. Diana watched as they made their way to the nearest chair. Boynton settled his companion, then fetched a glass of the waters.

Not until he was seated did he notice the two women. Then, with a hurried word to his aunt, he rose and came across to them. "An unexpected pleasure, to see you so soon again," he said. He saw Amanda's glass. "You're not drinkin' that awful stuff?"

Amanda nodded without enthusiasm.

"You'll be sick," was his blunt reply. "Seen it a hundred times. It only helps if you're already half-dead."

Seeing that Amanda did not appreciate this information, Diana said, "Is that your aunt?"

Boynton indicated that it was.

"And have the waters helped her?"

"She's forever coddling her insides with some nostrum or other; the waters are no worse."

His uncaring tone made both women gaze at him with disdain. "She looks as if she had been very ill indeed," said Amanda, who looked rather green herself.

"She always looks so," answered Boynton. "By the by, I have had some good news from London." He did not wait for them to ask what it might be, which was lucky, for neither was about to do so. They were directing pitying glances toward his unfortunate relative. "A few of my friends may toddle down later in the spring," he told them. "Seems London's dashed dull." He paused. "Of course, Bath is worse, but I shan't tell them that because it won't be once they arrive. Most sportin' set of fellows you could meet." He looked down as if conferring a particular favor. "Lord Faring, you know. And five or six others. Quite a party."

But Amanda and Diana had been diverted. Awed, they had watched Lady Overton struggle up from the chair where her nephew had left her and progress slowly but majestically toward them. She looked, thought Diana, like a massive ship under full sail.

"Ronald," she said now, in a tone that made all three straighten and Boynton start visibly.

He turned at once. "Oh, Aunt Sybil. Have you finished your dose? Care for another?"

Diana and Amanda exchanged an amazed glance. The change in Boynton's voice was complete. His air of slightly weary superiority had vanished, and he sounded like a schoolboy who abjectly hopes he will not be caned, but expects that in fact he will.

Lady Overton merely surveyed the group. Her eyes were very keen in her broad face, Diana saw, and she began to revise her opinion of the lady's plight.

Apparently the older woman found them acceptable, for her next words were, "Do you intend to present your friends to me, Ronald?"

Boynton actually flushed. "Oh. Of course. Aunt Sybil, Mrs. Trent and Miss Gresham."

Lady Overton nodded. Amanda and Diana had already risen, and they murmured greetings. "Will you take my chair?" offered Diana.

"No, thank you. We must be going. My doctor says I must walk as much as possible." Lady Overton's expression suggested that she found this advice unpalatable. "Come, Ronald."

"Yes, aunt," said the dandy in a cowed voice. Diana suppressed a smile.

Lady Overton took his arm, leaning on it rather more heavily than she really needed to, Diana thought, and they started to turn away. At the last moment, her ladyship looked back over her shoulder. "You should lie down, young woman," she told Amanda. Then, gripping so tightly that Boynton showed a distinct list to her side, she moved away.

"Well." Diana laughed. "There is some justice after all. She is precisely the sort of aunt Mr. Boynton deserves. How George will enjoy it when we tell him! And I had imagined her as such a despised, neglected creature. We must invite her the next time Boynton wishes to come, Amanda."

"Yes." But Amanda did not laugh. "Diana, I think perhaps I should go home now. I . . . don't feel well."

Diana turned at once. Indeed, her friend was terribly pale and seemed unsteady. "My dear, of course! Here is your shawl. Take my arm."

Though she would normally have rejected any such suggestion, Amanda did so. She was trembling, Diana found, and her hands were icy cold. Frightfully concerned, Diana led her toward the door.

"It must be the waters," said Amanda. "Mr. Boynton was right, it seems."

"We will get you a chair," promised Diana. "You'll be home in a trice."

"It is so ridiculous, but I think I would like to ride."

"There is no question about it." Arriving at the street, Diana looked around for an empty chair. Seeing one not far away, she signaled to the chairmen, and in another moment Amanda was settled inside. Diana walked beside the window, keeping an anxious eye on her friend. Amanda had leaned back, rested her head on the plush, and closed her eyes. She was still alarmingly white. Privately hoping it was nothing serious, Diana said, "Those waters would make anyone sick. You must not take any more, Amanda."

"I shan't! How can they call them medicinal?"

"Some people believe anything nasty is medicine. Only think of the dreadful messes we were given when we had the whooping cough."

Amanda laughed weakly, as Diana had hoped she would. They had been ill together as children, and Amanda had stayed at the Greshams' house in order to keep her sisters from infection.

"Here is the hill," she added. "We are nearly there."

The chairmen labored a bit going up toward the Royal Crescent. Diana slowed her pace to match theirs and wished they were home.

A tall thin figure emerged from George Street and turned toward them. Diana felt a flood of relief. "Captain Wilton!"

He looked up at once, and smiled, then frowned as he saw Diana's expression. "Is something wrong?" he asked, approaching.

"Yes, Amanda is ill. I am taking her home, but could you go ahead and warn them? A doctor should be sent for, I think, and . . . Oh, I don't know what else."

"Of course," he replied, concerned, and turned to go.

Only then did Diana notice his cane and remembered his injury. "Oh, perhaps I should go and you stay with Amanda," she blurted.

"Nonsense," was his only reply, and he set off at a rapid pace, swinging his wounded leg a little with each step but clearly quite able to hurry.

Diana breathed a sigh of relief, certain that she had put the problem in good hands.

" 'Op it, Jem," said the leading chairman. "The lady's sick like."

The men went faster. In ten minutes they reached the house and found its entire population waiting on the pavement for their arrival. George Trent looked nearly as pale as his wife as he hurried forward to help her from the chair. "Amanda! Are you all right?"

"Only a trifle queasy," she replied, trying to stand straight without swaying. "I foolishly drank some of the waters, and they have disagreed with me. I shall be fine in a little while, when I have lain down."

"I'll take you up."

"I can walk," she protested.

"Nonsense." And he swept her into his arms and carried her inside.

"I'll pay off the chair," said Captain Wilton. "You go ahead."

Diana walked in with the maids. "Has someone gone for a doctor?" she asked.

"Yes, miss. Billy went. He said one of the grooms next door knew of a doctor, for his mistress is sickly." The girl wrung her hands. "Will she be all right, miss?"

"Of course! Send the doctor up as soon as he arrives."

"I will, miss."

Diana ran up the stairs. She found Amanda lying on her bed and George sitting beside it holding her hand. "The doctor should be here soon," she told them.

Amanda started up. "Oh, I don't need a doctor. It is passing already."

"Nonetheless," replied George.

His wife sank back. "This is all so silly. It is my own fault for drinking those dreadful waters. They are such a cheat, George."

"Undoubtedly. Yet you weren't feeling quite the thing before, either." He grimaced. "I sometimes fear that living abroad has ruined your constitution, Amanda. And it is all my doing. I—"

"It has not! I never heard anything so ridiculous."

Amanda struggled to a sitting position. "Look, I am much better already."

George gently pushed her down again. "If you move before the doctor comes, I shall tell him you are a dreadful invalid."

She wrinkled her nose at him. "He would only recommend the waters, and then I *should* be."

They heard the bell below, and in the next moment the maid was ushering a kindly-looking older gentleman into the room. "Dr. Clark," he announced. "Your groom said I was wanted."

"My wife is ill," said George. "She took a glass of the waters, and they have disagreed with her."

Dr. Clark raised his bushy gray brows. "Indeed?"

"She is delicate," added George.

"I am not!" Amanda sat up again, defiant. "I feel much better already. I daresay—"

"Perhaps *I* should be the one to do that," the doctor interrupted, though so jovially that it could not offend. "I shall just examine you, since I am here, eh? And then we shall see."

"But—"

"If you will leave me with my patient." Dr. Clark indicated the door.

Diana went out. She left her shawl in her own bedchamber, then walked downstairs again. She would catch the doctor as he left, she thought, and find out his opinion.

"How is she?" asked Robert Wilton, coming out of the drawing room and into the hall.

"Oh, you startled me! I though you had gone."

"With Mrs. Trent so ill? But I am sorry I surprised you."

Diana waved this aside. "The doctor is examining her. He doesn't seem overconcerned."

"I daresay it is nothing."

"I hope so."

They fell silent, Diana too worried to chat and Wilton watching her face with compassion and admiration. The minutes passed. After a while, Diana looked up and said, "Oh, I'm sorry. I was thinking."

"It is not of the least consequence."

Grateful to him for refraining from meaningless chatter, Diana smiled. He responded, and their eyes held for a long moment, mutually appreciative. The exchange was broken only by footsteps on the stairs.

Turning, Diana saw the doctor. "How is she?"

"Quite all right," he replied. "A passing queasiness. She must stay away from our waters. They are not for everyone, you know. But there is nothing whatever *wrong*." He seemed to emphasize this word unduly, and his eyes were bright under the bushy brows, but Diana was too relieved to notice anything else.

"Oh, I am so glad!"

"Thank you for coming so promptly, doctor," said George Trent, who had followed him down the stairs. Major Trent was grinning.

"Happy to oblige." Dr. Clark took his hat from the maid, bowed slightly, and took his leave.

"I must go back to Amanda." George disappeared upstairs.

Diana let out a great sigh.

"You were very concerned about your friend," said Wilton.

"Of course."

He smiled. "I was about to send this. I may as well leave it." He held out an envelope addressed to both the Trents and Diana.

"What is it?"

"An invitation. I thought it wrong to call again on the same day, but the idea occurred to me, and I hoped to secure your consent."

"My . . ."

"All of you, that is," he added hastily.

"But for what?"

"An excursion to Beechen Cliff. A picnic, perhaps." Seeing her inquiring look, he said, "Have you heard of it? It is on the other side of the river, and the views are splendid."

"Ah."

"One can see the whole town, and beyond to the hills opposite."

"It sounds lovely."

"Will you come, then? Next week?" He leaned a little forward.

"I shall have to ask Amanda."

"Yes. Of course." But his face fell.

"I should like to, very much," Diana added, and she felt her heart beating faster.

Wilton smiled, blue eyes lighting. "Would you? Good."

"I'll speak to Amanda when she is fully recovered."

"Yes." There was a pause. "I should be going."

"Thank you for helping earlier."

He brushed this aside.

"And for the invitation." Diana felt elated but weary. The events of the previous hour had taken a toll.

Captain Wilton seemed to sense her fatigue. He simply bowed a little and said good-bye. When the door shut behind him, Diana moved automatically to the narrow window beside it and watched him walk away, his gait only a touch awkward from his wound.

The set of his shoulders and the small curls of brown hair at the back of his neck touched her somehow, and she went back up to Amanda clutching his invitation to her breast.

8

AMANDA WAS FULLY RECOVERED THE NEXT DAY. Indeed, she seemed in better frame than before. Captain Wilton's expedition was duly agreed upon for the following Wednesday, and that day dawned clear and unusually warm for April, to the host's great relief. Wilton fetched his party in a rented open barouche at midmorning.

Diana wore a new gown of white muslin sprigged with tiny dark blue flowers and trimmed with ribbons of the same hue. Ruffles at neck, wrist, and hem adorned the rather plain cut. She had threaded her straw hat with a matching length of ribbon, and rejoiced that she might leave off a pelisse in the mild spring weather, though George insisted that Amanda don one over her rose-pink gown. As they climbed into the carriage, the ladies gallantly awarded the forward-facing seats, Diana saw admiration in Wilton's eyes. A warm glow suffused her; she looked forward to spending an entire afternoon in Captain Wilton's company.

They drove down into the center of Bath, across the Avon, and up again on the opposite bank. The road soon became steep, and the horses strained in their harness. "Shall we walk, Wilton?" asked George Trent.

"We're nearly there."

And indeed, in a short time they turned sharply and came out onto Beechen Cliff, a parklike area above the town. "Oh my," said Amanda. "You can see all of Bath spread out like a map. Look, there is the Abbey Church tower."

"And there is Royal Crescent," responded Diana, pointing. "I believe I can see our very windows. What a splendid place!"

Captain Wilton looked gratified. He climbed from the barouche and offered a hand to Amanda. "Shall we walk about a little?"

The four of them strolled together for a while, exclaiming over various landmarks and praising Wilton's ingenuity in finding such a pleasant spot. But gradually the Trents dropped behind, Amanda leaning a little on her husband's arm. Diana did not even notice her friend's absence until they were a good distance off. Then she hesitated, suddenly very aware of her companion's muscular arm under her hand and his shoulder occasionally brushing hers.

"Aren't these fine old trees?" said Wilton, apparently feeling no constraint. "The prospect is particularly fine when framed by two branches, isn't it? Look there." He indicated a vista between two of the great oaks.

Diana agreed, at the same time telling herself that she was being silly. George and Amanda were still in sight. The proprieties were fully satisfied. Yet she had not been alone with Wilton since their first encounter, when her feelings had been far different.

"Ah, it is good to stroll again," continued Wilton. "There was a time when I feared I never would."

Diana's preoccupation with herself evaporated. "You are not using your cane! I did not notice until just now."

He smiled down at her. "No. I left it behind for the first time today. My knee is improving rapidly now." He stopped and flexed it slightly to demonstrate. The movement was stiff, and his face showed some discomfort, but it was mixed with elation.

"So this outing marks an epoch," laughed Diana. "We should celebrate it somehow."

"It does indeed." His blue eyes were serious as they met hers, and Diana had the feeling that he was speaking of something other than his leg. She drew a slightly shaky breath at the message he seemed to convey. "For the first time, I am nearly reconciled to my wound. I cannot help but regret being absent from the army, yet if I had not been hit, I would never have come to Bath. That would have been a tragedy indeed."

"It is a lovely place," agreed Diana, feeling the response banal but unable to think of a better one under his intense gaze. Her heart was beating very fast.

"Far more so than I had ever imagined," he replied.

He seemed to wait for some sign from her, and Diana was anxious to give it. But her tongue was suddenly clumsy. Once again she felt her inexperience, and the unfortunate effects of years of solitude. A young woman of five-and-twenty should not be so awkward, she told herself miserably. Captain Wilton would certainly expect more assurance than her blush. She made a great effort. "I had high hopes for this visit when we left Yorkshire. But they have been far surpassed."

"Ah." His face shifted slightly, the intensity a little eased by relief. "It appears we feel the same, then."

Diana raised her chin and met his gaze squarely. "Yes."

Their steps had slowed, and now they stopped altogether as the two of them looked at one another. A current of understanding passed between them, establishing many things without words. Diana knew at that moment that she loved, and was loved in return, and she felt that a wonderful future was opening up before her, requiring only a little more time to blossom.

Wilton seemed to feel the same, for he said nothing more just then. He merely tucked her hand a bit more securely into his elbow and walked on, his expression content.

"You were wounded at Bordeaux?" asked Diana after a while, eager to learn everything about him.

"Yes." He laughed a little. "I survived the whole of the Peninsular War without a scratch, only to be hit at the fag end of the thing, when we had crossed into France. A ricochet, too, they tell me. Bounced off one of the big guns."

"I wonder what it's like," mused Diana, almost to herself.

"Stopping a musket ball?" He was surprised.

She smiled at her own foolishness. "I mean the whole thing, really. The battle, and afterward. How idiotic I must sound to you."

"No. But it is not a pleasant memory."

"I beg your pardon. I should not have—"

"What I mean is, I don't think you would thank me for recounting my 'adventures,' " he interrupted.

Diana shook her head. "On the contrary. I should like to know, if you do not mind talking about it."

He shrugged, as if uncertain about this himself, and paused. "The actual battle," he said slowly then, "is all right. Mine is a cavalry regiment, you know, and when with Wellington, I also fought with the cavalry. It goes so fast one's memory is a blur, with vivid flashes, like tableaux. I remember a mount rearing and falling, an infantryman lunging with his bayonet, a friend standing in his stirrups and brandishing his saber for a charge. The rest of the time, you simply labor. It becomes automatic; your arm moves, you direct your horse to the thick of it." He shook his head. "The waiting beforehand is far worse to me because you have time then to imagine all the horrors that might befall you and your men, you see. And of course, after, being wounded . . ." He shuddered.

"Was it very dreadful?" asked Diana softly, though she knew the answer from his face.

"It was the worst thing I have ever endured," he replied, seeming hardly aware of his listener any longer. "My sergeant picked me up and got me away from the fighting to a wagon. From there it was as I imagine hell must be. We rode for hours in that infernal jolting cart, the sun burning us up and the motion making wounds gape for the flies. We thought ourselves saved when we reached the hospital, but that was the worst of all. It was rank with fevers, and the room where the surgeon examined my knee was ankle-deep in blood; a pile of severed limbs higher than my head stood in the corner. I thought he would take my leg, but the stench and the sights were so vile that I fainted as I tried to plead with him to leave it." He drew a long shaky breath. Diana pressed his arm, her gold-flecked eyes wide with horror and sympathy, and he looked down at her for a long moment, his expression quite blank. Then suddenly he came to himself and realized what he had said. "Good God! I . . . I beg your pardon. I forgot myself. I have never repeated these things to anyone, not even Trent, who no doubt saw worse. I don't know what possessed me to say them to *you*. I haven't the brains of a—"

"I'm honored that you did so," Diana broke in. "It is flattering to receive such confidences."

"*Such* confidences," he echoed bitterly. "You should not be subjected to scenes so terrible."

"You were," she pointed out.

"Yes, but I am a soldier, trained to hardship and bitter necessities. When it is necessary to fight for one's country—"

"You are always saying that no one should ignore the war," Diana interrupted. "If more people heard such stories, they could not."

"You are right." But he looked uneasy. "Yet despite my arguments, I cannot wish it. It is enough that soldiers bear these things. Those who can should remain . . ." He hesitated, looking down at her. " . . .unburdened."

"Yet burdens are often lighter when shared."

Wilton shook his head as if to dismiss her statement, yet he silently admired her compassionate heart.

"And if one is cut off from great chunks of a person's history, one can never really know him, or . . ." Diana broke off. She had been about to add "love him."

Captain Wilton smiled a little. "So each must tell his direst experiences? I am not convinced. But since I have inadvertently done so, is it not your turn now?" His smile widened, as if this were a good joke and a welcome change of topic.

Diana froze. For an endless moment it felt as if her heart had stopped. Though he thought he was jesting, she *did* have a history, one that would shock him more than his had her. She had pushed the past from her thoughts, blithely plunging into love with this man and looking forward to an idyllic future without considering its implications. What if he found out? Gerald Carshin was presumably still alive. He lived in London, or had lived there. Her secret was not safe here, as it had been in Yorkshire. She was, perhaps, even obliged to reveal it herself. What would he do if she acquiesced to his proposal and told? Diana looked up. His feelings would change, she thought. He might understand, sympathize, but she knew the world's reaction to those who had made such a mistake.

"What is it?" asked Captain Wilton. "You're white as a sheet. Are you ill?"

"I . . . I fear I am, a little," she murmured, feeling herself a coward.

"It is my fault! Why did I not mind my wretched tongue? Come, we will find the Trents, and go home, if you like."

Diana protested, but feebly, allowing him to believe that his stories of the war had made her faint. Under any other circumstances she would have scorned such an accusation, but now she was only too grateful for the diversion from questions about her past. What was she to do? she wondered, visions of a rosy future crumbling in her mind.

They found George and Amanda under a great oak tree not too far from where they had left their carriage. But another vehicle now stood behind it, and two young men were adding the finishing touches to a linen-covered table beneath the branches. "Captain Wilton, this is magical," exclaimed Amanda. "What have you done?"

"Simply engaged the kitchen of one of the hotels to provide our picnic," he replied with a brief smile. "My landlady did not feel her staff up to it. But I fear Miss Gresham is not feeling well."

Amanda stepped forward. "Really? Diana, what is it? Headache?" One of the waiters so far forgot himself as to look openly dismayed as he set a platter bearing an entire cold roast chicken on the table.

"No, no. It is nothing," she protested. "I merely felt a little tired for a moment. I am quite all right now."

"It is all my doing," added Wilton ruefully. "I have been telling Miss Gresham stories about the war." Seeing George Trent's surprised look, he said, "You cannot think me any more foolish than I do myself, George. I don't know what possessed me."

Amanda looked from one to the other of her companions as if uncertain what she should do.

"I tell you it is nothing," repeated Diana, anxious to dismiss this subject. She moved forward. "The table is lovely. It *is* like magic."

And certainly the scene Wilton's servitors had created was entrancing. Shaded by the oak tree was a square table covered with a snowy cloth that dropped almost to the grass. Four chairs were pulled up to it, and it was set with cutlery and china adorned with varicolored spring flowers. Flanking the roast chicken, which made a splendid show, were a round of yellow cheese, a brown loaf with a dish of butter, half a sliced ham, pickles and relishes, and, the crowning touch, a carefully arranged pyramid of glowing fresh peaches, their delicate hues seeming sunlit even under the tree.

"Where did you procure peaches?" wondered Amanda as they all gathered around the feast. "It is so early in the year."

Wilton looked at the other waiter, who answered, "From southern Spain, madam," causing Amanda to let out an ecstatic sigh.

"If you are sure you are all right . . ." said Wilton to Diana.

"Of course."

"Then?" He held a chair for her.

Diana sat down, as did Amanda opposite her. The gentlemen took the remaining seats. Wilton signaled, and the younger waiter came forward with a bottle wrapped in a white cloth and four crystal goblets. Deftly he set the latter before them and poured.

"Champagne!" cried Amanda, clapping her hands with delight. "Captain Wilton!"

"I thought we might dare a little," he answered, then held his glass aloft, its facets and pale effervescent contents sparkling. "A toast to the future," he added, "to victory in Belgium and to our happiness when the war is at last won."

They all raised their goblets, George cordially approving, Amanda almost tremulous with happiness, and Diana smiling but sick at heart. This was all so beautiful, she thought. The exquisite prospect of Bath spread out at her left; the nearer scene was perfect, and the spring air was so soft and mellow, but she no longer felt she belonged. The moment with Wilton had called up a host of old feelings and memories, those she had resolutely suppressed when she left home. And she saw now that she was here on false pretenses. Even Amanda thought her one thing when she was really another. It had been wrong of her to hide her past. She ought to have given her friend some hint at least before accepting her generous hospitality. Now it seemed too late, and the issue was further complicated by Robert Wilton, whom she had not foreseen. Had she imagined she would fall in love, she might have considered the implications, but she had unthinkingly grasped at escape without considering the effect on others.

Selfish, she accused herself, but this did no good now. She must think how to undo the tangle she had made in the way least hurtful to those she loved.

"Diana?" said Amanda softly.

Diana started. She was still holding her goblet high, while the others had drunk and set theirs down. She made a dismissive gesture and followed suit, turning to watch Captain Wilton and George, who were conferring over the chicken.

"No, no," Major Trent was declaring. "You're the host, Robert. It's your job. I shan't lift a finger."

"But I'm no hand at carving," he replied, holding the long knife as if it were some alien instrument. "I've managed a bird or two in Spain, but no more."

George crossed his arms on his chest and shook his head, adamant.

"Well, you'll advise me, at least?" asked Wilton.

Major Trent allowed that he would do that much, and the captain bent to his task. "I suppose I can start here." He inserted the blade between the chicken leg and body.

Trent gave a tiny cough.

"No?" Wilton looked up.

"I'd, er, start at the . . . er, front," murmured George.

"The front?" He turned the platter, trying to remain unaware of the amused scrutiny of the waiters, who had withdrawn somewhat until they should be needed again, but were well within hearing. He angled the knife against the breast.

The major nodded. "Slices, you know. The ladies will like those."

"Ah." Captain Wilton attempted to thinly slice the chicken. The result was rather thick and uneven, and he contemplated it ruefully.

Amanda burst out laughing, throwing her dark head back, then guiltily bowing it and covering her mouth. "I'm sorry," she said with a gurgle. "I truly am. It is just so . . ."

"Ridiculous," finished the host, torn between complete agreement, a desire to join her laughter, and a wish to appear poised and knowledgeable before Diana. "The last time I carved a chicken, I used a saber," he added.

"If I'd only thought, I might have brought George's," Amanda replied unsteadily. "It is sitting in plain sight in the dressing room."

The four exchanged a glance, the vision of Wilton attacking the chicken with his sword clearly in all their minds, and then they began to laugh. Even Diana could not resist the picture, and she found that the shared levity lightened her mood as well. She would find some solution, she decided, and until she did, she would not brood.

"Come, George," said Wilton, holding out the knife. "You must do it after mocking me in this callous way."

"Nonsense. You are going on splendidly," retorted the major with a grin.

Shaking his head, Wilton began again, and eventually, the bird was acceptably dismembered, and they ate their meal.

"Have you ever known anything so pleasant?" sighed Amanda after a while. "It is like the best of Portugal and England rolled into one. We are al fresco, and the food is wonderful, and there is not the least chance a troop of bandits or ruffians will appear over the crest of the hill and send us fleeing."

"Not unless the starched-up dowagers of Bath discover what we are up to and charge en masse," agreed Wilton.

"You think they would not approve of dining out-doors?" inquired Diana with a smile.

"I'm certain of it. When I was arranging this party, one elderly woman assured me that we would all take our deaths of cold, if not worse." He tucked his chin back and spoke in a fruity but stern voice. "Nothing is more deleterious than sitting still out-of-doors, young man. I thought everyone knew *that.*"

They all laughed again.

"She was wide as a house and looked sick as a dog herself," finished Wilton. "I nearly asked her if she had personal experience with the dangers, but it seemed too unkind."

"She sounds like Lady Overton," said Amanda to Diana.

"Someone remarkably like her," Wilton replied.

"Who is that?" asked George.

"She is Mr. Boynton's invalid aunt," Diana added.

George looked surprised, and slightly displeased at the mention of Boynton. "Not how I pictured her, really."

"She is not at all!" said Amanda, and told them the story of their encounter with Lady Overton. Before she was half-finished, they were laughing, and both men seemed very gratified by the end.

"Serves him right," said Wilton. "Puppy!"

"I just wish she kept him on a tighter leash," agreed Major Trent. The ladies groaned at his pun.

The captain turned to Diana. "When you next see—"

"If you call him my friend again, I shall throw this peach at you," she threatened, brandishing the fruit she had been peeling. Wilton drew up an arm in mock fear. "I know him no better than the rest of you."

The captain found this so gratifying that he forgot

what he had been about to say, and even George Trent seemed pleased.

"I am going to put my peach in my champagne," declared Amanda. "Have them fill my glass, George." She held it out imperiously.

He instead took it from her. "No more for you. You're rowing with half an oar as it is."

"I am not!" Amanda was indignant. "I am only happy." She threw out her arms and leaned back in her chair.

"Umm. Time to be packing up, I think, Wilton."

Amanda straightened and frowned, making it apparent that her high spirits were not due to over-indulgence. "George!"

He gave her a significant glance. "I'm merely being cautious, my dear."

Amanda seemed to recall something, hesitated, then agreed. "I suppose you're right. But surely we can finish our peaches."

They did so, then lingered a little while as the sun moved down the western sky. It was nearly four before they rose and reluctantly moved toward the barouche again. "What luxury," said Amanda, watching the waiters move forward. "We needn't even think of what to do with the three peaches remaining. It will all be whisked out of sight for someone else to worry over. I think we should always dine so."

"It might be less pleasant in the rain," suggested her husband. "Or in the winter months."

"Fustian!" she retorted, but she pulled him down beside her in the forward seat when they had climbed up, and rode homeward with her hand tucked into his arm and her head on his shoulder.

Diana, sitting beside Captain Wilton and very

conscious of his proximity, watched the Trents with wistful indulgence. How lucky they were, she thought, despite their misfortunes. If she could be half so happy . . . She glanced sidelong and found Wilton smiling down at her. A warm glow enveloped her, and she promised herself that she would find a way to secure such happiness for both herself and Captain Wilton.

9

A SERIES OF DAYS PASSED QUICKLY BUT HAPPILY FOR the Trent party. As May began, it became apparent that they would remain in Bath for an unspecified, but substantial, length of time. George was content making the rounds of military friends visiting the town, which was a constantly changing roster, always full of the latest war news, or at least fresh opinions. Amanda was obviously and luminously happy, though less strong than Diana remembered. Often she would not emerge from her bedchamber until noon, and then only to establish herself on the drawing-room sofa to read and write letters until George should come in and suggest a sedate drive in their hired carriage. Diana was thrown more on her own resources as the visit lengthened, and her long walks were usually solitary, with one of the maids trailing behind.

And yet she was not unhappy. Her fears of the picnic day gradually receded, as nothing came of them. She and Captain Wilton seemed to have reached a tacit understanding. Though nothing was *officially* settled between them, everyone appeared to take it for granted that it would soon be. He would make an offer, and Diana would accept, and all would be well. Wilton seemed content to leave it thus for now, and Diana certainly was. This situation allowed her to reap the benefits of an assured future without facing the responsibilities an actual offer would entail. She needed to decide what to tell him of her past. Indeed, Diana turned aside the beginning of a proposal, and Wilton, after a moment's puzzlement, allowed her to do so. For he, too, had his concerns. His knee was nearly healed, and the war was by no means ended.

But though Diana thought she was the same as ever, in fact she was far quieter and less apt to chatter to Amanda about things seen on her walks or laugh over some eccentric observed in their infrequent visits to the Pump Room. Robert Wilton, absorbed in his own plans and only newly acquainted with Diana despite his deep feelings, did not see it, but Amanda did. At first, she put it down to love. Diana was no doubt concentrating her liveliness and laughter on the captain, she thought, and it was only natural that she should see less of her friend, and that Diana should be serious, pondering the approaching change in her state. But as time passed and Amanda watched the two lovers together, her puzzlement returned, redoubled. They were a subdued pair, she could not help but think. She remembered vividly the culmination of George's courtship of her. When they had become officially engaged, and even just before, they had been nothing like this; their every moment together was a dazzle of sensation and confidences exchanged. She had felt she lived only in his presence then.

She told herself that their more sedate behavior was a consequence of age. She and George had been only nineteen and twenty, and these two were five or six years older. But this explanation merely made her sad, without convincing her in the least. She had seen love bloom at fifty in precisely the same breathless way. Amanda determined that she must talk with Diana and try to discover what was wrong.

But this was more difficult than she had imagined. Diana was so often out that it was not easy to catch her at a time when they might talk privately. Her walks grew longer and longer, until the maids began to protest and, as Amanda feared, Diana began to leave them at home and slip out alone. Too, Amanda did not always feel up to pursuing her active friend. She had been overtaken by a delicious lassitude in these days, and often a morning would pass without a thought of anything but her own rosy future. At last, however, she forced herself to rise particularly early one morning, and caught Diana at the breakfast table.

Diana seemed amused by her heavy eyes and sleep-puffed face. "You are up betimes," she said with a smile when Amanda entered. "And you do not look as if the morning pleases you."

"Is there tea?" was Amanda's only response. She was finding it impossible to gather her thoughts.

"There is." Diana poured, and Amanda added a generous dollop of milk and drank, both hands curled around the cup. She finished it quickly and gestured for more.

Laughing, Diana complied. "Why did you leave your bed, if you are so tired still?"

Amanda sipped her second cup more slowly, and even felt able to nibble some buttered toast. "I wished to speak to you," she answered, "and I never find you home when I rise late."

"But you should have simply asked me to stay. Is it something important?"

Realizing that she had made a mistake in her half-dazed condition, Amanda pursed her lips and tried to rally. "No, no. I meant only that I wanted some talk with you. We scarcely seem to see one another lately."

"Oh." Diana smiled again. "Well, you have grown so

lazy, Amanda. I cannot sit about the house all day. I am surprised you can."

"Perhaps I have a reason." She saw a way to explain her uncharacteristic appearance. She had meant to tell Diana her news for some time anyway, but had postponed doing so, reveling in her secret happiness.

Diana looked contrite. "I know. You have not been feeling quite the thing. I am the greatest beast in nature to have forgotten. Why do you not have the doctor again? Perhaps he can help."

"It is not a case of illness, Diana." Amanda flushed a little and looked down at her hands. "I . . . I am in an interesting condition."

"An . . . ?" For a moment Diana was mystified, then light burst upon her. "You mean . . . ?"

"Yes. I am going to present George with an heir. Or at least, so he insists. I shall be happy with a girl. *This* time." She smiled tremulously, awaiting congratulations.

But Diana was remembering an earlier confidence. Amanda had told her of previous tragedies in this area. No wonder her friend was being so careful. This new knowledge explained many things that had puzzled and sometimes irritated Diana. She felt relief mixed with guilt for her incomprehension. "That is wonderful!" she exclaimed, trying to put all her affection for Amanda into the phrase.

"So you see why I must not exert myself." A shadow passed across Amanda's pretty face. "I must be more careful than some."

"Of course you must!" Diana reached out and grasped her hand across the table. "And I shall help you. You must let me."

Amanda laughed at her vehemence. "How?"

"I can take over some of your household duties, and allow you to rest more."

"I have hardly any duties as it is, and you would hate talking to the cook, Diana. You needn't worry. I know what to do, and we are not abroad this time, so I need not ride when I am feeling ill, or eat odd messes." The shadow appeared again, then vanished. "I feel splendid." She looked at the piece of toast in her hand, swallowed, and put it down. "Most of the time," she amended. Her face paled.

"Are you ill?" cried Diana. "What may I get you?"

"It is nothing. It often happens. No need to worry." Amanda pushed back her chair and rose. "Excuse me."

Diana jumped up also. "I will help you upstairs!"

"No, no." She managed a laugh. "If I had known you would be worse than George, I would not have told you."

"Is there nothing I can do?"

"Wait for me," replied Amanda, and rushed from the room.

Diana found this a very difficult task. She went to the drawing room and paced back and forth, anxious about her friend's condition. More than once she started toward the stairs, but Amanda had insisted she wait, so she came back each time. Diana was even less experienced than most girls with such matters. Indeed, if Amanda had not been such a good friend, and if they had not been sharing lodgings, she would probably not have been told until the situation was obvious. She was gratified to be included, but also slightly uneasy. How could Amanda endure this illness, and how did she maintain her spirits with the losses of the past hanging over her? Diana's admiration for her friend rose another notch. She vowed to do everything she could to help her.

"There," said Amanda, coming into the drawing room barely three-quarters of an hour later. "That is over. Now I shall have some Madeira and biscuits." She went to the bell pull and rang.

Diana stared at her. She showed no signs of sickness; indeed, she was positively blooming.

Amanda turned from speaking to the maid and laughed at Diana's expression. "It passes off quickly. And it only comes in the morning—just at first. There is no need to look like I have risen from my deathbed."

"You are amazing."

"Nonsense." The maid returned with a tray, and Amanda poured out a small glass of Madeira and bit into a biscuit with appetite. "Now, is everything all right with you, Diana?"

"What?" She was still staring.

"We have hardly spoken alone in a week. Tell me what you have been doing."

Gradually recovering from her surprise, Diana recounted her walks and other activities.

"Captain Wilton has called nearly every day, I believe?"

"Yes. He came walking with me twice. His knee is hardly stiff now."

"You are glad to see him?" Amanda watched her face from under lowered lashes.

"Yes, of course."

Her tone was so unforthcoming that Amanda hesitated, but she could not leave the subject yet. "Has he . . . spoken?"

Diana turned her head away. "Of marriage, you mean? No."

"But—"

"It is really such a trivial question, is it not?" she burst out, rising and walking toward the front window.

"I mean, there is the war, and your news. I don't see why we must hurry."

"But do you not want to have your future settled?" asked Amanda gently.

Diana shrugged without turning, gripping her elbows in her hands.

"What is it, Diana? Do you find you do not care for Captain Wilton, after all? There is no need for you to think of him if—"

"No!" It was a heartfelt cry, and silenced Amanda for a full minute.

"What, then?" she said finally.

Diana came very close to telling her. They had shared so much in the past weeks, and now, this morning, the most intimate information of all. But the thought of Amanda's reaction stopped her. She had no doubt her friend would be sympathetic. She would say all the proper things about youth and naiveté and the impossibility of guarding against plausible villains when one has no family support. But she would still think Diana had been a fool, or worse, and she would regretfully conclude that such a mistake could not be simply erased. Probably she would say that Robert Wilton must be told before they were engaged. And her high opinion of Diana would be forever altered; she would not despise or revile her, of course, as others might have, but she would never admire or respect her quite so wholeheartedly, Diana felt. And this she could not bear to contemplate. "Nothing," she replied, attempting a light tone. "Except perhaps that I have been used to living alone, and it is sometimes hard to have so many people around me."

This wounded Amanda a little. "I thought you were happy with us."

Diana winced, but thought a slight hurt was better

than the alternative. "I am. Very happy. But I require more solitude than most people, I suppose. It is all so different here, and with Captain Wilton . . ." She trailed off, leaving Amanda to draw her own conclusions.

"Of course, it is a great change, though you seemed happier at first. And to think of marriage after being alone so long . . ." Diana bowed her head as if agreeing, and felt dreadfully guilty. "You do care for him?" added Amanda. "Because you know you are welcome to stay with us as long as you like. You needn't rush into any . . . other arrangement."

Diana swallowed a lump in her throat and blinked back tears. She felt wholly undeserving of such kindness. "I do," she managed in a choked voice.

"Well, then . . . I suppose everything is all right." But Amanda sounded unconvinced.

Diana longed to pour out everything then, but she still held back. The risk was too great. Silence fell and stretched as both women thought over what had passed between them, each wondering if something else did not need to be said.

But their tête-à-tête was over. The bell rang, and the maid came in to announce Captain Wilton. Diana moved from the window back to the sofa, and Amanda sat up straighter. Their smiles were a little stiff.

But Wilton was too excited to notice as he came striding in. "Letters from Belgium," he cried, waving a packet in the air. "I've had a great bunch all at once. They went to London, and my idiot of a brother waited to send them on until there was a pile." He looked around. "Where is George?"

"Out riding, I think," said Amanda. "He usually is at this time of day."

"But he must hear." The captain gazed about again,

as if his wish could summon Trent from thin air.

"He should be back soon," offered his hostess. Wilton nodded, disappointed. "Will you sit down?"

"No." He went to the window and looked out.

"Is there some great news?" asked Diana, exchanging a smile with Amanda at his restlessness. "The newspapers had nothing to say this morning."

The captain turned, and seemed to decide not to wait. "Nothing that we did not know," he said. "Except that the battle, the decisive battle, must be soon." He laughed a little, to himself. "It can't be much longer now. God, what I would give . . ."

The ladies watched him. He seemed far away, even though they sat not ten feet from him. Wilton's blue eyes clearly looked on a wholly different scene, and the animated lines of his body were ready for action. Unconscious of their scrutiny, he flexed his bad knee several times. Then, still looking out the window, he cried, "There is George!" and turned to go to him.

In the doorway he paused, a trifle shamefaced at his rude desertion. "My friend Buffer says the Belgian foxes are too stupid to live. Won't run." And with this he was gone.

Diana and Amanda laughed, but only for a moment. Wilton's excitement had had an adverse effect on them, somehow, and they sat in silence, straining their ears as he met George in the lower hall and began an eager recitation of his war news.

10

GEORGE TRENT WAS ABOUT THE HOUSE LESS THAN usual in the next few days, and Captain Wilton called seldom and seemed distracted when he did visit. They were easily found, however, in the Pump Room, or the concert rooms, or on a street corner, huddled with other military gentlemen discussing the progress of Wellington's and Blucher's joint effort in Belgium. As May passed, the excitement grew almost palpable among this circle. The mere idea of talking of anything else was ridiculous, and when Amanda or Diana tried a different subject, the gentlemen grew abstracted and took refuge in random nods and grunts. But if they were asked about the coming confrontation, their eyes lit and the conversation became almost overanimated.

"I wish it were over," sighed Amanda one day as she and Diana sat alone in the drawing room. "Of course, I have wished that many times these eight years, and that George could think of something besides fighting." She sighed again. "That is unfair of me to say. He often does—did—think of other matters. Only just now . . ."

Diana nodded, fully in accord with her.

"Ah, well, they say it can't be much longer. I should be grateful we are awaiting it here instead of in the field."

"Amanda!" Diana feigned deep shock.

She put a hand over her mouth. "If George heard me! All he wants is to take ship for Brussels. Do not tell him I said that."

"As if I should. Don't be a goose."

"I know it seems cowardly, but we were with the army so long, you see, and it is so hard to wait and wonder whether one's husband—"

"Amanda! I was roasting you. I am completely on your side. George has fought long and well. He should leave it to others now, and be thankful he got through it with only . . ." She hesitated.

"Only losing his eye, yes," Amanda agreed. "I have thought a great deal about that, and I do think it is better than losing a leg or an arm. George does not always believe it, but look at Colonel Peterson. He will always use a crutch, and . . ." She frowned and shook her head. "How did we begin such a dismal subject? You are right. George has done enough. So has Captain Wilton—nearly eight years at war. I wish they could see it so."

"It is unlikely to matter how they see it," replied Diana. "They are settled in Bath."

"Yes." Amanda sounded unconvinced. "But does it not seem to you that they are plotting something lately?"

"Plotting?"

"Since Captain Wilton received those letters from Belgium, whenever I come upon the two of them suddenly, George starts and looks guilty."

"I haven't noticed anything."

"Perhaps it is only my fancy. I hope so." But her expression remained concerned.

The sounds of hooves in the street and the front door opening heralded the arrival of the major. He nearly ran up the stairs and strode into the drawing room with shining eyes. Diana was abruptly struck with the improvement of his appearance during these last weeks. She had somehow overlooked it until now, perhaps because he had lacked the present air of eager elation. George Trent's color was normal again, and his great frame had filled out. Now the black patch over his eye was indeed rakish rather than merely pitiful, and he might have sat for a portrait of the pirate hero of romance.

"Amanda, I must speak to you," he said.

Diana rose to go.

"No, no, Diana. Stay. This concerns you as well."

Surprised, she sank down again.

But having gained their full attention, the major seemed reluctant. "Well, the thing is, Amanda," he began at last, then stopped again, shifting from foot to foot.

"George! Is it bad news?" his wife exclaimed.

"No, no. That is, I don't think so." He seemed to gather courage. "Wilton and I, and a few others, are going up to London tomorrow to see about returning to duty."

Amanda went very still, dismay plain in her face.

Seeing it, the major hurried on. "It's intolerable sitting here while the war is finished, Amanda. Most of us have devoted our lives to this fight. We thought we had seen it through. We deserve to be in at the end."

Diana saw that Amanda could not speak. "Do you not rather deserve a rest?" she asked, trying to give her friend time to regain control.

"Rest?" George seemed astounded.

"You have done so much," she added, less confident in the face of his obvious incomprehension.

"Do you abandon an important task when you

decide you have done 'enough'? Whether or not your job is completed? No." He shook his head and turned back to Amanda. "Can you understand?"

"You mustered out," she murmured.

"When I thought it was over. And with this eye." He grimaced, then recovered. "But that is changed now. And Wellington needs men. Wilton thinks there's a chance."

"Does he?" Amanda sounded forlorn.

"Yes. He is slated for duty in London, you know. But he is applying to Wellington himself. Friend of his family."

"But, George, I cannot go abroad," she answered with a catch in her voice. "You know I must be careful just now. Before, when I rode or . . ." She paused and cleared her throat.

"Of course you cannot," he said. "You will stay home this time, Amanda, and take care of yourself." Seeing her chagrin, he added, "I know it is said to be very gay in Brussels, but the army could move at any time. And I consider the balls and parties quite out of place anyway. I daresay I shan't be away long. And when I come back, the war will be over, and we can truly plan what we shall do and where we shall settle for good."

"You will leave me alone, in my situation?" Amanda could not help but say.

"No, no," he responded eagerly. "That's the beauty of it, you see. Diana is with you now. You needn't go back to Yorkshire; I know you get lonely there. And it won't be as it was when you stayed in London. You are settled here; you have friends. You might even have your parents for a visit. You will scarcely know I am gone."

"Oh, George!"

He had the grace to look ashamed, like a small boy who knows he has gone too far in arguing for a special treat. "Well, no, of course we shall miss one another. But they say the war cannot last the summer, Amanda. I'll be back long before you are brought to bed." He glanced at Diana, flushed a bit, and hurried on. "I *must* do this, love."

Amanda had risen and moved toward him; now she scanned his face. "Must you?" she asked wistfully.

George nodded, a little guilty, but determined.

"Very well."

He strode forward and swept her into his arms. "Darling! I knew you would understand."

"You won't leave from London, though? You will come back and say good-bye?"

"Of course."

Diana left them then, to discuss the matter more intimately, and went up to her bedchamber. Only now did she have leisure to consider that Captain Wilton was also leaving Bath, perhaps forever. Surely he would come to her first, she thought. But what would he say? The various alternatives that occurred to her were all unsettling.

Perhaps fortunately for her peace of mind, Diana did not have long to ponder the possibilities. Wilton called about an hour later, and asked for her. She received him alone in the drawing room.

"I wanted to be certain George had broken the news," he said. "I came as soon after him as I dared."

"Letting him absorb the heavy fire?" asked Diana with a smile. She had picked up a number of military terms in the last few weeks.

"From Mrs. Trent, yes. You may let fly at me when ready."

His smile was so engaging that Diana felt her throat tighten. She didn't want him to go; yet she dreaded the approaching exchange.

Her face seemed to encourage the captain, and he moved closer. "I wanted to say good-bye, of course. But even more, there is something to be settled between us."

"Settled?" She did not even recognize the high squeak as her own voice.

Wilton hesitated, a bit puzzled. He had often found Diana puzzling recently. Though he was certain she cared for him, she seemed to draw back whenever he made a move to deepen or confirm their relationship. He had not touched her, though he had wanted to, because of this, trying to give her time and room to adjust. But now, circumstances forbade waiting. "You must know what I mean," he went on. "Indeed, I am sure you do. We have understood one another since the picnic, though we have said nothing."

Diana looked at the floor, biting her lower lip.

"I love you," he finished simply. "And I hope you will consent to become my wife."

This was the moment she had dreaded. It was the proper time to tell him her secret and allow him to withdraw if he chose. Diana wanted nothing more than to say yes, but she felt it unfair to do so without revealing the truth. She could not so deceive him. Yet to be honest was very likely to lose all chance of happiness. The conflict made her tremble with anxiety.

"What is it?" said Wilton, seeing her distress but unable to guess its source. He tried a lighter tone. "You must say *something*, you know. It is extremely impolite to ignore a proposal of marriage."

Diana gazed up at him, the love she felt mingled with

pain in her dark eyes. Her throat seemed frozen; she could not speak.

Still not understanding, but responding to the appeal in her gaze, Wilton stepped forward and slid his arms around her, pulling her close so that she might rest her head against his shoulder. His hand rose automatically to stroke her deep gold hair, and the embrace seemed exquisitely right to him. "It's all right," he murmured, though he did not know what "it" might be.

Gradually Diana's trembling stopped. She felt a vast sense of safety and comfort descend upon her, and the question of her past receded slightly. What if she never told him? she wondered. It might not matter. His caresses lulled her into optimism, and she raised her head to meet his eyes. Her mouth shaped the word "yes," though no sound emerged.

Wilton gave no sign of hearing, but he bent and kissed her very gently, his lips merely brushing hers. Diana curved her arms around his neck, and he pulled her closer, molding her body against his and kissing her more urgently—once, then again.

Diana felt a passionate response rising within her, and she wanted nothing more than to hold Wilton tightly to her forever. Yet this new and charged sensation was confused by her dilemma, and, she was disgusted to find, by memories of the only other occasion in her life when she had been similarly embraced. Unbidden, the image of Gerald Carshin formed in her mind, enacting scenes of the foolish illusory love she had felt for him. Her tepid, uneasy reaction to Carshin's touch interfered with this very different feeling. She strove to push the memory down, but the mocking recollection would not be banished, and finally pulling herself away from Robert Wilton, she began to tremble once again.

"Yes," said the captain in a shaken voice. "I beg your pardon. I . . . I rather forgot myself." He was breathing rapidly.

Diana made a dismissive gesture.

He straightened his shoulders and smiled. "I can take that as my answer, with pleasure, but I should like to hear you say it as well."

"I . . ." She still could not speak.

"Isn't it odd how an offer of marriage ties one's tongue?" he said. "I thought I should never get it out. And yet we talk together easily about all sorts of other things." He took her hand and bent a little to look in her face. "Diana?"

"Couldn't we . . . just leave it until you come back?" she choked out.

He stared at her for a long moment, then murmured, "I am the most selfish beast in nature."

Diana was startled. "What?"

"To ask you to make this decision when I am about to go off to battle, where anything may happen. I suppose I didn't think of it because I have been so lucky in the past. But there is no telling whether I shall come out of it as I am, or . . ." He paused. "You are right, of course. We will not speak of this again until I return."

"That is not what I meant!" she cried, appalled that he should think this.

"There is nothing wrong—"

"It isn't!"

He met her eyes, and nodded. "Well, I'm glad *I* thought of it, then, for the idea is sound." He grinned. "I warn you I *mean* to return unscathed, however, and *soon.* So you must be ready to give me your answer then." He raised his free hand and very lightly stroked her hair again. "I was just so eager, you see."

"Oh, don't!" Diana threw her arms around his neck and buried her face in his coat. She had been so absorbed in her own worries that she had not even thought of his being hurt, perhaps even killed, in Belgium. The possibility tore at her heart, and she held him fiercely, as if to prevent his going.

He returned the embrace gently, then put a hand under her chin and raised it to kiss her lightly before stepping back. "You really needn't worry. My friends insist I lead a charmed life. And now I should go, for I have several things to do before leaving Bath."

"You will come back before you go abroad?" asked Diana, hearing herself echo Amanda.

"Yes."

She reached out to him again, and he took both hands. "I've handled this badly, and I'm sorry . . ."

"You haven't! It is I who—"

He laughed, putting two fingers over her mouth. "In any case, we will settle everything properly when I return. And I shall see you again soon, after London."

"I didn't . . ."

But Robert Wilton shook his head and turned to go, and Diana could not bring herself to voice her one wish: that she would marry him today if he liked, and follow him to Brussels or to the ends of the earth. Her desires were not in question, but Wilton's possible revulsion upon finding out her secret sealed her lips.

11

MAJOR TRENT AND CAPTAIN WILTON DEPARTED WITH their friends the following morning, high-spirited as boys going adventuring. Amanda was quite cast down when they had gone; she remained by the window for some time after they had disappeared toward the London road, chin in hand, close to tears. And Diana was at first too preoccupied to cheer her. She could not decide if she was more glad or sorry that Wilton had gone. Diana knew she would miss him, but his absence conveniently postponed difficult decisions, for which she still had no resolution. She welcomed the chance to push the questions aside. This was cowardly, she felt, but better than forcing confrontation. She would have a little more of the enjoyment and frivolity which had been so rare in her life thus far, before she had to withdraw once again.

For this now seemed the most likely outcome to Diana. She would go back to Yorkshire. No one had bought her father's gloomy house; it awaited her there, its contents as yet intact. After her brief taste of gaiety, it would receive her again as if nothing had happened. In her more despondent moments Diana felt that perhaps Yorkshire was where she belonged. Each time she had ventured out, she had botched things; probably her father's teaching had made her unfit for society and the sort of loving home Amanda had established.

Part of her recoiled in horror from this prospect, and urged her to dare all to grasp happiness. But it had to combat a fatalistic voice that had been nourished by years of solitude and contemplation of her mistakes. It was far easier for Diana to convince herself that she had made a mull of things again than to rouse the energy to fight.

It was scarcely a question of battle in any case, she reasoned. If she, like Wilton, had been riding off to face an enemy with saber and pistol, she might have managed. The prospect was daunting, but conceivable. But Diana had no weapon with which to fight the disgrace that would engulf her should Wilton learn of her past. Rather than a snarling adversary, she would confront a lover, and watch him turn, not into an enemy, but something distant and disapproving. The thought made her shudder.

And so she made a great effort not to think of it. She turned her attention resolutely to Amanda and exerted herself to keep her friend amused and comfortable. Since Amanda's physical condition was as delicate as her emotional state—she was still often ill in the morning and tired during the rest of the day—the task was engrossing, and Diana found she could forget her own troubles for hours at a time.

"We should go out today," Diana insisted on the third morning after George's departure. "You cannot mope about the house this way. You always took a drive before, remember. You need fresh air."

"With George," was the melancholy reply.

"Yes, well, you will have to make do with me now. And he will be back before you know it. Indeed, he is to return in two days' time, if all goes well. You do not want to greet him all pale and languid, do you?"

This had some effect. But Amanda was not easily rallied. "He will be going away again almost at once."

"Perhaps. However, there is one thing we have not considered, Amanda."

"What?"

"The army may refuse to take him back. He did fight long and hard, and he has lost an eye."

Amanda, who had been reclining laxly on the sofa, sat up. "Oh, do you think there is a chance?"

"I do, though never tell George I said so."

"He would be furious," she agreed, sitting straighter still. "I suppose I am a horrid selfish cat, but I hope you are right. Particularly if the fighting is not to last long this time. It seems so silly for him to go."

Diana nodded, thinking that it really was very likely the major would be refused. Captain Wilton was another matter. "Why don't we go to the concert tonight?" she suggested then. "You enjoy the music, and it would not be strenuous. You can keep to your chair the whole time, if you like."

Amanda considered. "All right," she answered slowly, as if unable to find a suitable excuse for refusing.

"Good. And this afternoon, we will go for a short drive. You really are looking wan, Amanda."

This also was allowed, and after dinner that evening the two women set off to the concert rooms—if not exuberantly, than at least with a calm contentment. Amanda wore a gown of primrose muslin and really looked much better for her drive. Diana had chosen an amber sarcenet that was nearly the same hue as her hair, worn with some amber beads that were her mother's only legacy. They arrived just as the musicians were striking up and slipped into seats near the back.

Diana was pleased to see the tight lines in Amanda's face relax a little as the music began. Her friend was fonder of music than she, a fact that had influenced Diana's choice of activity for tonight. Gradually Amanda leaned back in her chair, bowed her head, and half-closed her eyes.

Amanda's enjoyment ensured, Diana was free to look about her. The room was fairly full, as there was no assembly this evening, and she saw a number of Trents' acquaintances dotted about it. She also glimpsed Ronald Boynton and his aunt near the front, evidently part of a large party. As she watched, Boynton leaned across his massive relative and spoke, quite loudly, to a brown-haired man. A dowager in purple just behind him glared through her lorgnette. With a slight smile, Diana composed herself to listen.

At the interval, Amanda was almost cheerful. "This was a splendid idea, Diana," she said. "You were very right to insist."

"Would you like something? Tea? I'll go and get it."

"I'll come with you," said Amanda, half-rising.

"No, no. There will be a great crush in the refreshment room. You wait here."

"But you should not go alone."

Diana was amused. "What could happen to me here? I'll just be a moment." And she moved off before Amanda could protest again.

It was indeed very crowded, and Diana was subjected to several quizzical glances as she made her way through the press. It was customary for the gentlemen of a party to fetch refreshment for the ladies. She ignored the stares, however, and slowly moved closer to the viands. When at last she had procured tea and cakes, and was picking her way back with a small tray, she heard her name called. But as she recognized the voice as Ronald Boynton's, she did not even pause. Let him think she hadn't heard.

Mr. Boynton was not easily discouraged. He repeated his call, and in the next moment had hurried forward to confront Diana. "Miss Gresham!"

"Oh, how do you do? You must excuse me, I am just taking this tray back to Mrs. Trent."

"My friends have arrived from London," he replied, oblivious of her excuse and not offering to take the tray. "Nearly the whole group. Is it not splendid?"

Nodding without enthusiasm, Diana tried to make her way around him.

"You must come and meet them. They are prodigious fashionable, you know."

His pleased excitement might have amused Diana under other circumstances, but just now she was simply annoyed. "I cannot. I must deliver this tea. If you wouldn't mind stepping out of the way?"

"What?" He became aware of Diana's burden for the first time, and this awareness brought with it the knowledge that he should come to her aid, though he clearly did not wish to.

The succession of emotions visible in his face made Diana smile, but she was weary of waiting. "Let me pass, please."

"Er, certainly. I, er, I must . . ."

She didn't linger to hear his excuses. Slipping between two chatting groups, Diana left the refreshment room.

"I'll bring them round to meet you after the concert," she heard Boynton call after her, but she paid no heed.

The interval was nearly over by the time she reached Amanda, and they drank their tepid tea in silence. Amanda seemed to enjoy the second part of the concert as much as the first; she was smiling and humming softly when they rose to go. Diana, on the other hand, was preoccupied by the thought that she must get someone to fetch their carriage, though all available servitors were besieged by others with similar desires. It was much more comfortable, she realized, to go out with a gentleman who took responsibility for such details.

"I am afraid we may have to wait a little," she told Amanda. "Everyone is trying to leave at once."

Amanda nodded, and they withdrew a little from the crowd at the doors.

"There you are, Miss Gresham," exclaimed Ronald Boynton, bearing down upon them from the concert rooms. "Did you forget that I promised to present my friends to you?"

In fact, she had, and she found herself wishing that he had been equally forgetful.

"Some of the most elegant folk now in Bath," he was telling her confidingly. "You won't wish to miss the chance. Nor will Mrs. Trent, I vow." He nodded to Amanda, who looked amused. "Lord Faring is among them," finished Boynton, as if offering them a great prize.

This did pique Diana's curiosity a little. She would not object to meeting Robert Wilton's older brother, she thought. She would be interested to see what he was like, though she already knew that he did not much resemble the captain.

Boynton took her hesitation for eagerness. "Just come along this way," he instructed. "We're waitin' within until the crush eases."

Diana glanced at Amanda, who shrugged, and they allowed Boynton to usher them through an archway and back into the concert rooms. "He reminds me of a cat we once had," whispered Amanda very softly. "She was forever bringing me the mice she caught, and dropping them at my feet."

Diana stifled a laugh; the comparison was perfect, and the treat Boynton promised seemed nearly as distasteful.

"Faring," Mr. Boynton cried, and a slender brown-haired man ahead of them turned. "Like you to meet some of my Bath acquaintances." He gestured.

"You are wrong, Amanda," murmured Diana. "*We* are the mice." And indeed Boynton seemed pleased to be presenting such a pretty girl to his noble crony. He performed the introductions with a complacent smirk.

"Enchanted," said Lord Faring, bowing over Diana's hand. She would never have known him for Wilton's brother, she thought. Their coloring was the same, and an informed observer could trace certain similarities in the lines of Faring's face. But in every other respect, the brothers were clearly opposites. Faring's dress was the height of dandyism, and his countenance showed evidence of years of excess in its pouchy eyes, premature lines, and lack of color. He surveyed Diana with an appreciative insolence that made her wish to turn her back.

"Miss Gresham is a friend of your brother's," added Boynton.

"Indeed?" Faring seemed to find this amusing. He spoke in the same drawl as Boynton, but more languidly. "You must not judge our whole family by the gauche Robert. His years abroad have left him ignorant of everything except shooting, I believe."

"On the contrary," answered Diana coldly. "I found

him remarkably well-informed. And he is a valued friend of Mrs. Trent's husband, Major Trent.''

"Ah." Again Lord Faring seemed amused.

Boynton was not yet done with introductions, however. He reeled off the names of several other gentlemen, and finally, hailing another who came up just then, said, "And last of all, but by no means least amusin', Miss Gresham, my friend Gerald Carshin.''

Diana had already begun to turn, and Amanda was facing the newcomer. The latter was a fortunate circumstance, for Amanda's polite response covered Diana's frozen immobility and allowed her the necessary instant to force herself to resume movement. She did not, however, recover her composure, and she faced Gerald Carshin in wide-eyed silence.

He, too, was patently startled. But his self-possession, or perhaps effrontery, was greater. "Miss Gresham and I have met before," he murmured, and bent to kiss her limp hand.

"I might have known," joked Boynton. "You always know the pretty girls, Carshin. Where did you meet?"

Carshin did not answer, but this was evidently not unusual. "How are you?" he asked Diana.

She tried to speak, and failed, the implications of this encounter boiling up in her mind.

Amanda sensed some strangeness in her friend. She looked sidelong at Diana, then at Carshin, and said, "We must be going, I'm afraid. We were waiting for our carriage."

"We will escort you," offered the newcomer. "Boynton here can send for your vehicle." Adroitly he slipped Diana's hand into his arm and started off, leaving the group a bit nonplussed.

"If he is not the most complete hand," Boynton was heard to murmur.

"Do you call it that?" responded Faring, who was obviously used to more deference.

One of the other men, recalling his manners, offered his arm to Amanda, and the rest of the party followed toward the exit.

"You are as lovely as ever," said Gerald Carshin to Diana. He could feel her trembling on his arm, and he rather enjoyed the sensation.

Diana was silent; she was gradually recovering from the shock, but she was not yet up to conversation.

"You seem unchanged, in fact, though it has been . . . what, seven years?" Carshin had not thought of her in nearly that long, but now details were coming back to him. Had it not been seven years until Diana came into her fortune? "I see no ring on your finger?" he ventured. "You have not married?"

"No," she managed.

"Ah." Carshin's brain began to work. His financial position was no better now than it had been seven years ago. If anything, it was worse; the charity of such as Lord Faring, who was by no means a leader of fashion, kept him afloat. And he had had no luck in attaching another heiress whom he could imagine as his wife. The reappearance of Diana Gresham, obviously not in disgrace with society, seemed providential. And I objected to coming to Bath, he thought with a shake of his head. "Nor I," he said in a melancholy tone that sought to imply he had never gotten over her.

Diana understood it, and the audacity of the man made her stare up at him in amazement. He tried to look soulful, and succeeded merely in impressing her with the change in him since they had parted. Diana remembered Carshin as a blond Adonis. He had indeed been handsome; moreover, such a memory partially explained her foolishness in her own eyes. She had been dazzled. But the man she saw now was scarcely dazzling. His pale hair was thin, and an incipient paunch strained his waistcoat. The weight of years of hard living stamped his features—a hint of jowl marred his clean jaw, and his blue eyes gazed out from a network of tiny wrinkles.

"Perhaps it was fated thus," he went on, throwing her another intense look.

"Fated?" Diana was nearly herself again.

"That neither of us should be attached, and that we should meet again after all this time."

"I can't believe the fates so stupid," she replied tartly, not really believing him serious.

"To keep us apart so long?" Carshin realized that she still resented the past. Only to be expected, he supposed, though she seemed to have retained her position in society. But he had his work cut out for him. It was fortunate that he enjoyed a challenge and that the prize was so worth the effort.

"To bring us together at all."

He bent a little toward her, not enough to cause comment, but so that he could whisper in her ear. "Too hard! You cannot have forgotten those golden days when we first met. The tulips I brought you? Our walks over the moors?"

A luminous haze did lie over those recollections, Diana realized. Though she had bitterly deplored her own stupidity at seventeen, she had concentrated on the elopement itself. The preceding time retained some of its magical aura.

"I was a fool," murmured Carshin. "Worse! But I have been sorry for it ever since. If you knew how I regretted—"

"So much that you could not even write," she interrupted.

"Exactly. I was afraid to write to you. I knew how you must despise me. A thousand times I began a letter, only to tear it up in despair."

For a fleeting moment Diana almost believed him. Her active imagination pictured the scene he described. She had known enough to despair herself to be reluctant to judge others. But then she met Carshin's eyes, and the illusion dissolved. At seventeen she had been blind to the calculations and self-love mirrored there. At five-and-twenty, she was not. There had been no letters, and no regrets. Gerald Carshin had probably not thought of her from that day to this unless— Diana's heart froze with her next thought—he had told their story to his cronies, to amuse them. Briefly, she couldn't breathe; then she realized that none of the other men had seemed to recognize her name.

"But now I have been given the opportunity to make amends," Carshin was saying. "I can scarcely believe my good fortune. I will show you how—"

"No." she looked at him, coolly appraising. "I don't wish to see you again; please do not speak to me."

He paused, weighing various replies. "Surely you would not be so unforgiving as to—"

"It has nothing to do with forgiveness. I simply don't like you, and I don't wish to associate with you." This bluntness felt amazingly good. Diana drew in a breath, pleased.

"Do you not?"

"No." She withdrew her arm. "If you will excuse me,

I must see about the carriage and join Mrs. Trent."

"I wonder what your friend Mrs. Trent would think if she knew the story of our . . . association? Apparently you kept it secret somehow, but that need not go on."

Diana stared at him, appalled.

"Ah, that catches you up, does it? Perhaps there are others who would be interested in the story." Seeing her expression, he added, "Perhaps some whose good opinion you value even more highly, eh?"

"You—"

"Now, now, don't say anything you'll be sorry for later." He stepped close again. "You will see me, and speak to me, and do as I tell you. For if you don't, all of Bath will hear our romantic history." He grinned unpleasantly. "And your friends shall hear all the most intimate details." He looked her up and down in a way that brought back that night they had spent at the inn. Diana flushed crimson.

"You horrible . . ."

He held up a warning finger. "What did I tell you about name-calling?"

She turned away, moving toward Amanda, and Carshin added, "So good to see you again, Miss Gresham. I shall certainly call tomorrow," in a voice that all could hear.

Once Diana and Amanda were safely in their carriage, Amanda, though weary, turned to her friend and asked, "Wherever did you meet that man Carshin, Diana?"

Diana looked away so that her friend couldn't see her expression. "He visited Yorkshire several years ago."

"Indeed? That must have been one occasion when you were grateful for your father's reclusiveness. The

man's manner is quite unpleasantly insinuating. I
hope he does not actually call.''

Gazing out the carriage window, Diana thought de-
spairingly that Amanda would never understand her
ill-fated elopement of years ago.

12

DIANA PASSED A DREADFUL NIGHT. THOUGH SHE HAD always known that Gerald Carshin could turn up, she had never really believed that he would. That episode of her life was so remote it seemed to Diana as if Gerald must have faded as well. Faced with his indisputable presence, and his threats of exposure, she was at first devastated. She saw no way to fight him, and the precarious happiness she had begun to embrace crumbled silently into nothing. Diana was not even certain that flight would save her, for Carshin knew her home and he might follow her there should she retreat to Yorkshire for a while. He was determined to have her fortune this time; she had seen that in his eyes. Nothing else she could offer him would slake that greed.

For a wild moment, as she tossed and turned in her bed, Diana considered trying to sign her money over to Carshin, on the condition that he never come near her again. But the idea died almost at once. The scandal would be nearly as great, and she did not really wish to lose all her wealth to such a cause. Carshin would probably not consent, in any case.

When the maid came in with early tea, Diana was awake; indeed, she had scarcely slept at all. Yet no plan of escape had come to her. She washed and dressed in a cloud of despair and went down to sit at the breakfast table alone and drink two more cups of strong tea. Amanda would not be down for some time, but Diana had no desire to take her usual walk. In fact, she had no desires whatever. She sat gazing blankly at the wall until the servants silently signaled that they must clear up.

She removed to the drawing room and resumed her pose, her mind utterly empty. Only the sound of carriage wheels below at midmorning roused her, and then not quickly enough to allow her to escape. As she reached the drawing room doorway, she heard footsteps on the stairs and knew that she would be seen leaving. Diana stood very still, trying to tell from the sound if it was Gerald Carshin. But would not the maid have announced him? On this reassuring thought, George Trent and Robert Wilton strode in.

"You're back!" she cried, her relief making her almost exuberant.

They nodded, unsmiling.

Diana gazed from one glum face to the other.

"It was no good," responded Wilton. "They turned us all down flat. Said there wasn't time to get us to Brussels even if we were completely fit, which we weren't."

"Damned paper-pushers!" exploded George. "What do they know about it? Where's Amanda?"

"In her room," said Diana.

Trent turned on his heel and went out without another word.

"I'm sorry," added Diana. "I know how much you wanted to go."

Captain Wilton nodded again, then shrugged. "I considered simply getting on a ship, but Wellington would more than likely send me back."

Diana couldn't think of anything really comforting

to say. And her own new dilemma dwarfed Wilton's problems in her mind.

"At least . . . I shan't be leaving Bath after all," he said after a while, with a valiant smile. "I hope you are glad of that."

"Yes. Yes, of course." But Diana's voice lacked conviction. How much better it would have been if he had been posted abroad, she thought. Perhaps somehow, in his absence, she might have found a solution to her problem and freed herself to accept his proposal when he returned.

"You don't sound so," he countered, half-amused, half-concerned. "Is something wrong?"

"No." Her tone was too vehement, she thought. Why could she not control her voice?

"Mrs. Trent is not ill?"

"No. She is quite stout. We went to a concert last night. Amanda enjoyed the music very much."

Wilton eyed her. Diana searched her brain for some remark that was both sensible and safe. But before she could think of one the recurring sound of carriage wheels froze her tongue.

"We returned as soon as we heard the army's judgment," said the captain, trying to put her more at ease. "There was no reason to stay, and we were both eager to be back. The journey went quickly."

Diana heard only the bell, the front door opening, and more footsteps. The maid knew that Captain Wilton was here; she would see no reason to turn away other callers. And Diana could hardly rush out and give those instructions now.

"Mr. Gerald Carshin, miss," said the servant, and Carshin strolled into the room, resplendent in yellow pantaloons and a pale blue coat.

"How d'you do." The newcomer was blandly cordial. "Miss Gresham. And Captain Wilton, is it now? I believe we've met at your brother's."

Wilton was clearly annoyed at the interruption, and by one whose posing he despised. But his emotions were nothing to Diana's; she thought at first that she might actually faint, though she would have scorned such a suggestion only days before. As she gathered her scattered sensibilities, and the two men surveyed one another, the contrast between them was graphic. Robert Wilton stood so tall and slender, his face cleanly etched and open, while Carshin was battling corpulence and irredeemably sly. The thought of the one telling the story of her past to the other made Diana feel ill.

"I dropped in to see if you would care to go for a drive, Miss Gresham," Carshin went on. "Pleasant day."

"As you see, Miss Gresham is occupied," answered Wilton.

"Indeed?" The other man looked about the room as if seeking the nature of this occupation.

Diana saw Wilton tense, and she cringed. "Perhaps another day," she offered, hoping to placate Carshin. The captain stared in amazement.

"But another day it may rain," insinuated the caller. "I think you would do much better to come now."

The command, and the threat, were patent. Diana did not dare refuse, especially with Robert Wilton standing by. Conscious of his outraged, incredulous gaze, she stammered, "Well, perhaps . . . I have not been out today, and . . . we will be meeting again soon, Captain Wilton."

"Do you mean to say you are going?" he demanded.

"That seems to be the gist of it," replied Carshin, an amused sneer on his face.

Wilton continued to look at Diana.

"I . . . I . . . It is a pleasant day."

Stiff with astonished anger, the captain merely bowed and turned away. He could not imagine what Diana was about. To put him aside for this coxcomb! It was beyond bearing, particularly after his defeat in London.

Diana, desperate, opened her mouth to recall him, but she did not know what to say. She was trapped, she thought, and she could no more loose herself than could the rabbit or the quail. The worst unhappiness she had left in Yorkshire was nothing compared to this.

Wilton was gone. Gerald Carshin smiled complacently and gestured toward the door. "Shouldn't you fetch your hat?"

Whirling abruptly, Diana almost ran to her bedchamber.

It was some time before she returned to the drawing room, but when she did she was once again in control of her feelings. Something must be done, she had decided, and at once. She could not endure more scenes like this morning.

Carshin was chatting with George Trent when she came in. The major looked thunderous. "Not a very pleasant fellow," said Carshin as they climbed into his hired carriage. "Deuced surly, in fact. You'd have thought I was a dunning tradesman or one of his wife's family putting the squeeze on." He laughed. "The eyepatch is a bit thick."

"Major Trent was wounded in the war," answered Diana coldly, "and he is not fond of dandies."

"Well, if he thinks me one, he's sadly out." Carshin seemed genuinely offended. "Even a soldier should be able to see that I don't indulge in their freaks."

It was true, she conceded to herself. His dress was not as exaggerated as, for example, Mr. Boynton's. But George would not see any difference.

"But we shouldn't be talking of him." He turned the carriage in the direction of the Sydney Gardens. "We have much to settle between us." He looked over at her, then turned back to the road. "You really are more beautiful than ever, you know."

"I don't want your compliments. Indeed—"

"Don't take that line." His tone was conciliatory. "Why be angry? I have apologized for my mistakes. Can we not be friends again? I really am sorry, you know." And he realized he was indeed sorry. It had been foolish of him to abandon this lucky find—a beauty and an heiress. He must repair his slip and get her for his own.

"I'm not angry," responded Diana. "What passed between us was over long ago. That is the end of the matter."

They had entered the gardens, and now he pulled up. "Shall we stroll a little?"

"No."

"Come, come. It is a beautiful day. What harm is there in a walk?"

Frustrated, Diana tried to think of some objection, but she had more important concerns. "Oh, very well!" She jumped down without waiting for him to help her, and refused to take the arm he offered.

"Would it really be so bad?" he asked as they walked along one of the paths. "To be married to me? I would be an exemplary husband, you know. I swear I should never give you cause for complaint. We would have our town house as we planned, remember?" He leaned a little toward her.

"I remember that you planned to set yourself up in town with my money."

"To set both of us up," he corrected. "I wasn't going to rob you."

"Were you not?"

"I can understand your annoyance. It is true, I was young and stupid. But I have learned better since then." He stopped and faced her. "Money is important. It is far easier to be happy in comfortable circumstances. You cannot deny that. But other things are equally important. That is what I did not see seven years ago." Before she realized what he meant to do, he had stepped forward and slipped his arms around her waist. "Seeing you again, all my old feelings returned. There is no one else I wish to spend my life with. Dare you claim it is not the same for you?" And pulling her close, he kissed her passionately.

Diana's few wisps of golden memory dissolved. Her calf love for Gerald Carshin had been wholly fantasy and foolishness, she saw now. Not only the elopement, but even the first meetings had been empty and vain, the intensity of feeling purely a product of her own loneliness and longing. Had she had the usual opportunities to meet young men, she would never have idealized Carshin. She didn't even like him, nor had she really then. She had been swept away, not by a man, but by her own airy dream. His kiss left her unmoved, except for distaste, and she realized that it had always been so. At seventeen she had had no standard of comparison. Having met and loved Robert Wilton, she could judge the true value of Carshin's vows and caresses. With all her strength she pushed him away.

Startled, Carshin staggered back. He had been certain he was about to win her over. He was rather vain of his success with women, though it had been mostly among those for whom money was a prime motive, and he did not put much stock in Diana's protestations. She had believed his avowals once; why should she not again? And when he held her, his intellect was overwhelmed by a rush of desire. She was so lovely!

Diana turned back toward the carriage. "I don't want to see you again," she said. "If you call at the Trents', you will be refused. And if you dare to touch me again—"

"Just a moment." He strode after her, enraged by thwarted desire, and grasped her upper arm, pulling her around. "You are forgetting one small matter, are you not?"

"Your threat to expose me?" In her anger, she nearly had. And she had determined to argue with him so coolly. "You would not tell a story so detrimental to yourself. The ruin and abandonment of a girl of seventeen would make you look despicable."

"You think not? There are many ways of telling a tale. And in any case, *I* should not come out the worse. You would be far more affected."

Diana pulled her arm free, but she did not turn again. "You could not be so . . ." Biting her lower lip, she tried to think of arguments to sway him.

"Alas, one is forced to distasteful actions sometimes." He eyed her. "I daresay Captain Wilton would find the story interesting, at the least. I have the impression you would not care for him to hear it."

She could not help but wince.

"I thought so. Perhaps he is the reason you will not listen to me, as you once did. A pity. But there it is. Can't say I think much of your new tastes."

"Stop it!" Diana clenched her fists. "I will give you money, if you will just leave me alone."

Carshin laughed. "It is not only your money I want, my dear Diana. I think you know that very well. Besides . . ." His smile broadened. "I shall get it all when we are married."

"I shall never marry you!"

He gazed admiringly at her blazing eyes and rigid figure. She really was a beauty. Even that outmoded way of dressing her hair seemed to contribute to her appeal. He was filled with greedy desire. "You shall marry no one else. I'll see to that. What other man would take you? Shopworn goods are not much in demand, m'love."

Burning with rage, Diana slapped him as hard as she could, then drew back, her palm stinging from the impact.

Carshin, an angry red mark rising on his cheek, grasped her shoulders and shook her a little. "Spitfire! You have changed, haven't you? But I know how to deal with such as you.' Crushing her against him so that her arms were pinned between them, Carshin kissed her savagely again.

Diana kicked at his legs and tried to jerk her head from side to side, but he was too strong, and she was trapped until he released her.

"There!" Carshin allowed her to move away. He was breathing quickly, and his blue eyes burned with determination and desire. "We shall not be bored, lovely Diana. What a life it will be."

Diana could not speak. She was awash with conflicting emotions: revulsion, rage, a desperate calculation.

"I see no reason why we should not announce our engagement at once. We can put it about that we are old friends meeting again after a time and confirming our long-standing attachment."

"I shall do no such thing!" Diana started toward the carriage again, walking swiftly.

In three strides he caught up with her. "I don't see that you have a choice."

Diana's hands itched to strike him again. If she had had a weapon, she realized, she could have killed him easily. This certainty further unsettled her. "Do your worst," she answered through gritted teeth. "I would rather be ruined than married to you. I lived alone in Yorkshire for seven years, I can do so again!"

Carshin, who would not have contemplated living in the wilds of Yorkshire for even seven days, had not counted on this, for he judged others' reactions by his own. "Here, now, no need to be so violent. Perhaps I have gone too fast. I see that I have. We will talk of this again."

"If you come near me again, I shall leave Bath and go home," she declared, though her heart sank at the prospect.

"You are overwrought. When you have had time to consider, you will see . . ." Carshin's voice trailed off as they reached the carriage. Diana quickly climbed up, pushing aside his assistance. When they sat side by side in the vehicle, she replied, "Understand that I shall never marry you, whatever you do. If you choose to spread the story of our elopement in spite of this, you will. But it will gain you nothing except my deeper contempt."

"And the satisfaction of seeing you prevented from marrying any other," he snapped, his temper overriding his common sense.

Diana merely turned her head away from him, her face like stone.

Regretting his words immediately, Carshin sought to make amends. "I beg your pardon. I did not mean that, of course. It is just that you have provoked me to—"

"There is nothing more to be said between us. Ever."

Gazing at her exquisite profile, Carshin experienced a deep pang of regret and anger. He refused to lose this prize when he held such a strong hand. She was angry now, and ready to say anything, but when she was cooler, the prospect of ruin would seem less bearable, and then he would try again. Pondering his next approach, he urged the horses forward.

13

DIANA DID NOT SPEAK A WORD ON THE DRIVE BACK, and she evaded Carshin's aid when she climbed down from the carriage and entered the Trents' house. She went straight to her room and flung off her hat and shawl, then curled up in the armchair before the fireplace and burst into violent tears.

Her confused emotions demanded such release, and it was some time before her sobs changed to sniffs and then silence. When she finally raised her head, breathing deeply, she felt better, though nothing had changed.

Diana stared at the floor and considered her situation. Though she would never marry Gerald Carshin, she dreaded the consequences. Despite her brave words to him, the thought of disgrace and her friends' shock and disapproval made her shiver. She had only just become accustomed to the warmth and small gaieties of society, and now they were to be taken from her. She could retreat and live alone; she did not doubt that. The years in Yorkshire had taught her much about her limits and possibilities, and she knew that books and daily chores would provide a bare minimum for existence. The breath of scandal could not touch a solitary.

But she wanted more. Now that she had seen something of life, and been offered love, she resisted losing it with all her strength. The thought that she would never see Robert Wilton again made her throat ache anew. Yet once he was told of her past . . . Diana clenched her hands in her lap and tensed as if preparing for a blow. There seemed no way out.

Diana's helplessness brought back memories of that earlier time when she had been abandoned by Carshin. Then, too, it had seemed that the world was against her, that she was wholly alone. Yet help had materialized, she reminded herself, and luck had swung her way after misfortune. Straightening, Diana allowed herself a small grain of hope. She could not see a solution just now, but all was by no means lost. She would not give up, as Carshin no doubt wished she would.

With this tenuous optimism she rose and washed her face. As she dealt with the wisps of deep gold hair that had escaped from the knot on her neck, she realized that she was extremely hungry. She had eaten hardly any breakfast this morning in her worry.

Diana found the Trents just sitting down to a buffet luncheon in the dining room. Amanda looked radiant, and George seemed to have recovered somewhat from his disappointment.

"There you are," said Amanda. "We were just about to send someone. What have you been doing this morning?"

"I went out driving."

"With that fellow Carshin," said George. It was not a question, nor, quite, a criticism, but the major's opinion was obvious.

"The man from the concert!" Amanda was surprised.

"Wilton seems to have left in a hurry," added George, and Diana raised her eyes to find that he was watching her closely. This was so unlike him that she at once concluded Captain Wilton had confided his intentions. She flushed slightly and dropped her eyes.

"Was he here?" exclaimed Amanda. "And he did not even say hello."

"You were not yet downstairs," replied her husband. "Though I thought he meant to stay awhile."

He was looking at her again, Diana knew. Misery descended on her once more. "I suppose he wished to get settled in his rooms after your journey," Diana offered.

The major merely grunted, and Amanda looked from one to the other of them in puzzlement.

"Will you go for a drive this afternoon?" asked Diana quickly.

"Oh, yes." Amanda smiled up at the major, who responded in kind. "To Sydney Gardens, I think. To see the flowers. You have walked there, haven't you, Diana?"

Struck dumb by mention of the scene of her morning's humiliation, Diana merely nodded. But she watched the Trents with a mixture of envy and sadness. They were so happy together; no dark secret hung over them. Despite the major's infirmity and his recent disappointment, he gazed at Amanda with love and contentment. And Amanda seemed a different woman from the languid, dismal creature of yesterday. They would never truly understand, Diana thought, if they were told her story. They would feel pity and regret, but she would become an embarrassment for them. "Excuse me." She pushed back her chair. "I believe I will go for a walk."

"So soon after luncheon?" Amanda looked startled. "Won't you sit with us a little first?"

Unable to form a polite excuse, Diana simply shook

her head and hurried out. Amanda turned to her husband, frowning. "I wonder if something is wrong. Should I go after her?"

"No." He hesitated. "Wilton loves her, you know."

"I thought he did." Amanda smiled happily. "Told me on the way home that they were practically engaged."

"Oh, George, that's . . ."

But he held up a hand. "Think something's gone wrong. Wilton didn't say so, but I'm fairly certain he meant to settle things between them this morning. No reason to wait now. I expected to find them when I came down, and to hear the good news. Instead, Wilton's gone off, and Diana sets out with this Carshin popinjay. Know anything about him?"

"Not really. He is a friend of Mr. Boynton's. We met him at the concert. Lord Faring was there as well."

"Wilton's brother? Ha." Major Trent fell into a a brown study, his brow furrowed. "Can't make it out," he added after a while. "Wilton thought the thing was certain."

"Perhaps he made a mistake? He may have taken something Diana said . . ."

"Not Wilton. He's not that sort. Not one for the ladies, you know." Trent shook his head again. "No, something's amiss."

Amanda looked distressed. "I must talk to Diana."

"Do that. She won't do much better than Wilton, you know."

She nodded absently.

George stood. "Believe I'll just stroll down to the Pump Room. See if there's any news. I'll be back soon."

"In time for our drive."

"Of course."

Amanda saw him out with a smile, then walked slowly into the drawing room and sat down. She could not imagine that Diana admired Gerald Carshin. Indeed, she knew that Diana cared for Captain Wilton. What, then, was happening? She hoped that Diana's walk would not be as lengthy as usual.

Diana, striding briskly along the high common, was no longer thinking of the Trents. She was trying not to think at all, in fact, for every line of thought led to unpleasant conclusions. She concentrated on the beauties of the budding June landscape and the pleasures of brisk movement. As always, walking was a relief.

It was impossible to keep her mind blank, however she strove to suppress its spinning. Recent events, and her dilemma, would surface, and then she would go round and round again, ending up at the same impasse. Carshin had the upper hand.

Diana paused to watch a group of children playing hide-and-seek among the trees; then she moved on, walking in a great circle that brought her back to the Royal Crescent at midafternoon. The Trents were out, as she had calculated they would be, and she had the place to herself.

But she had no sooner entered the drawing room than she heard the front bell, then hurried steps on the stairs. She turned, to meet Robert Wilton in the doorway.

"I had to come back today," he said. "I must talk to you."

Diana's heart turned over. He looked so handsome in his dark blue coat, his thin face worried and intent. As for Wilton, he was more than worried. He had walked off his anger during the hours since he left the Trents' house, and as it faded, fear had risen to take its place.

He had thought Diana his; now it seemed he might be losing her, and the idea was unbearable. Old insecurities arose when he considered his apparent rival, for Carshin was a town beau, his dress and manners those of the haut ton. Captain Wilton was accustomed to being thrust aside for such men; it had happened repeatedly in London. And though he had thought Diana different, her behavior this morning had shaken his opinion as well as his certainty of her affection for him. His first impulse—to throttle Gerald Carshin—was clearly unacceptable, but he had little faith in talk, his only recourse.

Now that he faced Diana again, no words came. He simply gazed at her, his blue eyes questioning.

"I . . . I am sorry about this morning," she murmured, looking down. What explanation could she possibly give him?

"It did seem . . . odd," he replied. "I very much wanted to talk to you."

"I know. I . . ." She searched for words.

"When we spoke before I left Bath, I thought . . ." He retreated a bit. "But I have been too precipitate. I have assumed things I had no right to assume. You must put it down to my deep feelings for you. And I hope you will forgive any—"

This was too much. "There is nothing to forgive!"

"No?" He bent to try to see her face. "Well, I am glad of that." Wilton paused, hoping she would volunteer some explanation of her actions. When she did not, he added, "This Carshin, you have known him for some time?"

Diana looked swiftly up, then down again. "Amanda told you?"

"No, my brother. Carshin is one of his friends, you

know, and I inquired when I saw Faring in the Pump Room today. It . . . was important to me."

"We met years ago. We have not seen each other since," she replied. Her heart was pounding, and she felt again like a trapped animal, beating on the doors of her cage, desperate for a way out. Diana wanted nothing more than to tell Wilton everything and throw herself into his arms. But she did not dare. She searched for a way to reassure him of her love without revealing the truth.

"Ah. He is very elegant, I suppose. Faring says the ton finds him charming." How his brother had enjoyed giving him this information, Wilton thought. His own fears must have been obvious, and Faring had always reveled in a superior position.

"Really?" Diana strove to sound blandly surprised. "That seems a bit strong."

"You do not?"

"No."

"Yet you were very eager to drive out with him this morning."

"I wasn't. I . . . I had said I would, and . . ."

"It appeared that he only then asked you."

Near tears, Diana turned away.

"Miss Gresham. Diana!" He put his hand on her shoulder and turned her back again. "You will say I have no right to interrogate you so, but—"

She shook her head. "It is not that. It is that I cannot answer you." And she began to cry.

At once he pulled her into his arms, cradling her head against his shoulder, a hand in her gold hair. "I'm sorry," he murmured.

Diana had never felt so comforted. His arms around her, his voice in her ear, were an exquisite relief. For a few moments it was as if all her cares were lifted from her shoulders. But as her tears lessened, the necessity to explain once again arose, and she pulled back.

Wilton offered his handkerchief, and she took it to wipe her eyes.

"Let us forget the whole matter," he said then. "I care less than nothing for Carshin, unless you do."

Diana shook her head again, miserably.

He smiled, his face lighting. "Well, then." He reached for her again, putting his hands on her upper arms. "You know how I feel. I have told you that I love you and want you for my wife. Now that my future is more settled, will you not give me your answer?"

She gazed up at him through tear-filled eyes.

"I should tell you that I have some little income besides my army pay. I had thought to retain my commission, but if you would prefer another sort of life, I am not averse. My war service is ended, in any case. I have a small estate in—"

"Stop!" Diana could not bear to hear him reciting his prospects, as if she were to judge him by such standards.

He waited, then added, "Will you not say something?"

She must, Diana thought, but she could not think what. She could neither accept nor refuse him—the first because of Carshin, and the second because she loved him dearly. The only proper course was to tell him her history, and that she was afraid to do. "I *want* to marry you," she stammered, and before she could go on, she was in his arms again.

For Wilton, all doubts and fears were swept away by that phrase. The terrible worry that she was lost to him dissolved, leaving in its wake such happiness as he had never known. His life opened out before him in myriad scenes of bliss: Diana in his arms, their children, their home together. He kissed her with a mixture of exuberance and passion.

Diana resisted halfheartedly for a moment. She had meant to go on. But her love for him soon won out, and she gave herself to the embrace. Her whole self seemed to rise up to meet his, and her arms slid automatically around his neck. It was some time before she even realized that the obstacles she had felt before were gone. The reappearance of Gerald Carshin, and his despicable behavior, had expunged him from her happy memories. No longer did his image intrude as Diana responded more and more eagerly to her love's caresses. She was free of the past at last.

But this very realization made her draw away, for she was not, in fact, truly free.

Wilton let her move only a little. His arms stayed about her waist as he laughed down at her, his eyes warm with love and desire. "We can announce our engagement at once. You must come to London to meet my mother. And there is no reason to delay the wedding beyond a month or so, is there? Oh, Diana, we shall be so—"

"No!"

He stood very still, looking down at her. "What?"

"I cannot marry you. That is . . . I . . ."

"Did you not say that you wished to?"

"Yes, but . . . there are things which prevent . . ." This was the moment to tell him, Diana thought. Perhaps she was mistaken; perhaps he would pass it off as unimportant now and feel just the same about her. But as she met his pained, puzzled eyes, she felt a shiver of fear. If the love there should change to withdrawal, she could not bear it.

"Has this something to do with Carshin?" he asked very quietly, his face growing hard.

Seeing it, Diana quailed. "Why do you . . . ?"

"There is nothing else it could be. Our situation remains the same, save for him." Captain Wilton's expression became almost grim, and Diana concluded that she had been right to hold back her story. But he was thinking only of the man who appeared to be preventing their happiness. Diana had never seen this side of Robert Wilton's character, for she had never seen him at war. Though she knew, of course, that he was a soldier and had fought for most of his adult life, this conveyed little to one who had no experience of battle. Her own fears led her to misinterpret his determination as disapproval, and she moved farther away.

Wilton let her. Indeed, he seemed withdrawn, his gaze inward. Diana almost cried out to him, terrified that she had lost him. In fact, he was merely shifting to another mode of thought, one he had never used in a drawing room before. He was sizing up Gerald Carshin as he would have a French army camped before his lines, examining his apparent weaknesses and planning a campaign. There was no question in the captain's mind that he would win, but since he was a first-rate soldier, he left nothing to chance.

"It . . . it is not exactly Carshin," blurted Diana. "It is me. Or, at least, both, in a way." She would tell him, she decided. Nothing could be worse than the way he looked through her now.

But Wilton brushed her efforts aside, engrossed in his plans. He needed more information, he thought, and at once. He could not move without better intelligence. And Diana was not the best source at this stage. Wilton straightened. "I must go."

"Now? I want to tell you . . ."

He smiled at her, and ran a finger down her cheek. "Everything will be all right. You needn't worry. I shall take care of it."

This silenced her. She could not imagine what he meant, or what he planned to do. "You don't understand," she answered finally.

"I understand enough."

"But—"

Abruptly he pulled her close again and kissed her, thoroughly but quickly. Then he stepped back and smiled again, almost jaunty. "Don't worry," he repeated, and with a sketch of a salute, he went out.

Diana, mystified, ran to the window and watched him move away along the street. Where was he going? To Carshin? She shivered and wrapped her arms around herself. Surely not, for he had looked almost happy. She debated running after him, but the preceding half-hour had drained her, and she could not face renewing that strain. Dejected, she went to the sofa and sank down, head in hands.

14

SEVERAL QUIET DAYS FOLLOWED, AND DIANA GRADually overcame her conviction that something was going to happen. She had written Captain Wilton a note on the evening after their encounter, asking what he meant to do, but he had put her off with a soothing, and uninformative, reply. Dispirited, she allowed time to pass without acting. Indeed, a kind of lethargy seemed to have descended upon her. She could think of no solution, so she left developments to fate.

Wilton, meanwhile, was very busy. He talked to a number of his acquaintances in Bath, wrote letters to London, and even questioned his brother about Carshin, so subtly that Lord Faring got no inkling of the focus of his interest. He found this campaign almost as satisfying as a true military action. By the beginning of the following week he felt he had gathered all the intelligence he needed. Though he still did not understand precisely what lay between Gerald Carshin and Diana, his greater knowledge of the man's character fostered theories, none of which made him more kindly disposed to his rival. He was nearly ready to act.

On a balmy afternoon in mid-June, Amanda Trent came into the drawing room in search of Diana. "A huge basket of flowers has arrived for you," she said. "It is beautiful. Come and see."

They went into the hall together, and Diana gazed at the tall bunch of roses and daisies.

"Aren't you going to look at the card?" wondered Amanda. She was watching her friend's face closely. Despite the Trents' growing preoccupation with the coming addition to their family, Amanda had noted Diana's low spirits and loss of vivacity. She and George had repeatedly puzzled over the apparent rift between Diana and Robert Wilton, but neither Amanda's inquiries at home nor George's outside it had yielded any substantial information. Amanda was determined now to discover the cause. "Is it from Captain Wilton, do you think?" she added.

Diana slowly reached for the small envelope thrust between the stems. If it was, she thought, she would only feel more guilty. Pressing her lips together, she tore it open. Then, with a disgusted sound, she dropped the card on the hall table and turned away. Amanda hesitated only an instant before picking it up. "Gerald Carshin," she read, frowning. "What can he mean by 'Will you not reconsider?' Reconsider what?" She replaced the card and followed Diana into the drawing room. She was standing at one of the front windows gazing out into the street. "Diana, what is the matter?"

"Nothing."

"Nonsense! You *will* tell me."

Diana turned, startled by the command in her friend's voice. She had never heard Amanda speak so sharply.

"It is obvious that something is wrong. And this Mr. Carshin is the cause, isn't he? Is he the reason for your quarrel with Captain Wilton?"

"We haven't quarreled."

"Call it what you will. Diana, he told George his plans. What happened?"

"I suppose half Bath knows by this time," Diana murmured, turning to lean her forehead dejectedly against the window glass. This was a foretaste of what her life would be like when the secret was out, she thought.

"Oh, lud!" cried Amanda. "I could just *shake* you!"

Again Diana turned, surprised.

"You have been mooning about in the most irritating way. You act as if it is too much even to say good morning. But when I try to help, you insist there is nothing the matter, or you moan that everyone knows. Knows *what*, Diana?"

Acknowledging the justice of Amanda's complaints, Diana came out of the window embrasure and stood straighter. "I cannot tell you."

"Indeed? And whom can you tell?"

"No one."

"Not Captain Wilton? Or Mr. Carshin?"

"He . . . I . . ."

"Diana, I cannot bear your moping much longer. It is driving me distracted!" Amanda Trent, though capable of similar behavior, was unskilled at standing idle while her friends suffered. She was much happier taking them in hand and doing something. Indeed, this impulse had been partly behind her original invitation to Diana.

Diana nodded. "I know. I have been a poor sort of guest these last weeks."

"You have!" Amanda smiled a little, but Diana did not look up.

"I think I should go home. That would be best for everyone."

"Home! To Yorkshire? You shall do nothing of the kind. I did not mean—"

"I know, but I have been thinking of it for a while. I can't see any better solution."

"To what? Oh, why won't you tell me?" Amanda's tone was pleading. "I have told you so many things. Are we not good friends?"

Diana felt torn. She wanted to confide, but she was still afraid.

"How can you simply shut me out?" added Amanda, her face showing real pain.

Bowing her head, Diana gave in. She could not stand against such pleas, particularly not when they urged her own inclination. Amanda would guard her secret, whatever her reaction, and her response would tell Diana something about how others would react. "I told you I met Mr. Carshin in Yorkshire years ago," she began.

"Yes."

It was very difficult to go on, but Diana forced the words out. "We were not mere acquaintances." And with gathering speed, the whole history of her elopement poured out.

When she finished, there was a long pause. Diana, who had kept her eyes on the floor through her recital, looked up to find Amanda frowning and biting her lower lip. Diana trembled a little as she waited to hear what she thought.

"You were foolish," said Amanda after a while.

"Yes."

"But you were very young, and you had no one to guide you. Your father was . . . so difficult."

Diana made no reply. She was trying to discover Amanda's feelings from her tone, without much

success. Her friend sounded more puzzled than condemning.

"And I suppose Carshin seemed charming," she
went on doubtfully.

"I had been allowed to meet no young men, and he
was practiced at seduction." She hadn't meant to
excuse herself, but she couldn't help it. "Oh, Amanda,
do you despise me now?"

"What?" Amanda looked up, surprised. "Of course I
do not. I have just been trying to decide why I am not
more shocked. I could never despise you. I feel I *should*
be shocked, but I am not, really. It seems the most
natural thing."

Diana stared at her.

"That you should have made such a mistake,"
Amanda explained. "If I had had such a father . . . But
of course there was George, and we . . . Yet I should
never have met him if I had not been allowed to go to
the assemblies . . . and in any case—"

She was cut off by a joyful embrace from Diana. "I
was so afraid you would think me sunk below
reproach!"

Amanda returned her hug. "You should not have
done it, of course," she said when they separated.

Diana laughed, weak with relief. "You need not tell
me. I have thought of little else during the last seven
years."

"That is why you were living alone in Yorkshire?"

She nodded.

"But did no one else know?"

"Only our housekeeper, and she kept the secret.
More from taciturnity than love for me, I think."

"Ah."

"I really am deeply sorry for my mistake. I have

repented it bitterly since that day. If I could make amends . . ."

"You have, I think. Seven years alone! You might as well have been in prison."

I was, Diana thought, but she said nothing.

"Besides, it is for Mr. Carshin to make amends. He behaved despicably; you were merely foolish."

Diana laughed again, without humor. "He wishes to; he wants to marry me, now that I have my fortune safe and sound."

Amanda opened her dark eyes wide.

"He is so eager, he threatens to drive off any other suitors by telling them the truth."

"He did *not?*" gasped Amanda. "Then that is why you and Captain Wilton . . . ?"

"Yes. You see the tangle I am in. And I am afraid to tell him."

Amanda did not have to ask whom she meant by "him." "Umm. Gentlemen feel rather differently about these matters," she murmured, imagining George's response to such a revelation.

"Yes," replied Diana miserably.

"Yet you cannot marry that . . . blackguard."

"I shan't. I shall go home first, and live as I did before."

"Oh, Diana! You love Robert Wilton, do you not?"

"Yes." Her face was bleak.

"You and he are such a good match. You would be happy, I know it."

There was no reply to this.

"We must think of something, make some plan!"

"I have thought until my brain whirled. I can see no way out. Carshin is implacable."

"But there must be a way." Amanda stamped her

foot. "I won't see you made unhappy now, after all
this. I will think of something."

Diana smiled a little, amused and touched by her
vehemence, though not optimistic.

"Just give me a little time," added the other. "I
often have quite good ideas."

"Of course you do."

"You think I don't, but you did not see me in
Portugal. I had to contrive the most astonishing
things at times. And I shall do so with this."

Despite her doubts, Diana was heartened. It was
wonderful just to have someone on her side, and
Amanda's certainty was contagious. Could there be
some way out, after all?

"Come and change for dinner," Amanda went on,
linking her arm with Diana's. "And do not so much as
think of the problem until tomorrow, after the
assembly. Leave it all to me."

Diana started. This was an unsettling echo of Robert
Wilton's words, and it made her uneasy once again.
But Amanda, in her exuberance, would not allow
Diana to brood. She swept her friend upstairs and com-
manded her to dress in a tone that elicited automatic, if
laughing, obedience.

Diana chose her gown carefully, for she knew the
assembly that evening would be an ordeal. Carshin was
sure to be there, as was Captain Wilton, and they
would be surrounded by a host of curious eyes. She
settled on a dress of deep gold satin, trimmed with
knots of gold-shot brown ribbon that had charmed her
when she discovered it in the dressmaker's shop. It
was a bit overformal for a Bath assembly, but the trim
echoed the hues of her eyes. She fastened an extra knot
of ribbon in her coif, and surveying the result, was
satisfied that she looked well, at least. The cut of the

gown, with a deep square neck and full puffed sleeves, complimented her unusual hairdressing, and her eyes seemed to sparkle with the glints of the ribbon. Fastening her string of amber beads around her neck, she took a last look, then went down to dinner.

The meal was dominated by military talk. George had gathered news in town after their drive, and he could think of nothing else. Napoleon's forces were advancing into Belgium, he told them, and a battle was imminent. All other concerns were driven from his mind by this one great issue, and he dominated the conversation with his speculations as to where the armies would meet, how Wellington would fare in his first real confrontation with Boney, and what Blucher's troops would do under the guns of the French. Amanda seconded him as best she could, and Diana joined in for the first part of dinner, but with the second course her thoughts drifted back to her own dilemma. The war was, she thought guiltily, more important, of course, but she could not seem to keep her mind off personal matters.

The dancing had already begun when they arrived at the assembly rooms, and they found chairs at the side as a quadrille was finishing. Major Trent deserted them almost immediately, saying, "There is Randolph. I must speak to him."

Amanda was philosophical. "I didn't really expect him to dance tonight. The news is too exciting. Let us move over there beside Mrs. Brown and her sister, so that I will have someone to talk with when you dance."

"I'll stay with you," protested Diana. "I don't want to dance."

"Nonsense," declared Amanda, rising.

"But, Amanda . . ."

The diminutive Mrs. Trent looked back and up.

"You must forget your troubles and have a splendid time. I insist upon it. Come." But her expression as they crossed the room was far from carefree, and when Gerald Carshin approached a few moments later to solicit Diana's hand, Amanda had to hide a grimace.

"I don't think I shall dance tonight," Diana replied to him.

"Not dance? But you must." His emphasis on the last word made both Diana and Amanda raise their chins defiantly. But Carshin would not be denied, and at last Diana followed him out onto the floor. As the music began, her heart sank; she had not realized it was a waltz.

Smiling as if he knew her thoughts, Carshin encircled her waist with his arm and swung her into the set. Diana, glancing up at him, then down, wondered miserably how she could ever have thought she liked this man. How different this assembly was from her first in Bath. Then she had been so excited and happy, thinking a new world was opening before her. Now things were even worse than before her escape from Yorkshire.

"You are very lovely tonight," ventured Carshin in his most ingratiating tones.

"I don't want your compliments," replied Diana coldly. "You forced me to dance with you, but you cannot make me talk."

Carshin cursed inwardly, though his smile did not waver. Since his last encounter with Diana he had been racking his brain for a plan to captivate her. Despite his threats, he did not really want to reveal their history to the world. For he wanted not only her person and fortune, he longed for the social position her money could bring. Those of the haut ton who now despised him as a mere hanger-on would come round quickly enough when he had a town house and carriage and an irreproachably suitable wife. Carshin wanted to sit in the bow window at White's, and be greeted with deference when he entered a drawing room. Diana could provide the necessary element—money—but it would be worthless if she were disgraced. Though he was careful not to let her suspect the truth, he was nearly as eager as she to keep their secret. He was determined to capture her as she was. At this point, he looked down, savoring Diana's curve of cheek, her glowing hair and skin, the rounded contours of her shoulders and neck. She was everything he desired, a damnably lucky chance at this point in his career. He would win her!

They turned in the dance, and Carshin's gaze encountered Captain Robert Wilton leaning against the far wall, arms crossed over his chest. The captain watched the dandy steadily, as a hunter does his prey, and for a moment Carshin was shaken. Wilton's eyes were so coldly calculating. Then his brief uneasiness was swept away by rage. The thought of any other man getting Diana made Carshin nearly sick with fury. He had unearthed this prize; it was his by right! And before he allowed anyone else near it, he would spread the tale of their elopement, and damn the consequences.

Wilton's mood was far different. Any anger or jealousy he might have felt at seeing Diana in the arms of his rival was submerged in his meticulous plotting of tactics. Tonight was to be his final observation. He wanted to see Diana and Carshin together once more before he decided what to do. And what he had seen so far merely reinforced his view of the situation. Diana had not wanted to stand up with the man; that had been evident to one who knew her well. He had some-

how compelled her to do so, and this confirmed
Wilton's conviction that Carshin had some power over
the woman he loved. At that moment, his soldierly
control nearly broke, but he quelled the desire to go
after the interloper with his fists by recalling his training. No sortie succeeded without planning and disci-
pline, he told himself, and returned to observation.

Carshin was a devious opponent, Wilton decided as
the waltz continued. Such a man would never attack
openly; he would try to manipulate or maneuver.
Indeed, in his world, this was the rule. But that made
him all the more vulnerable to a frontal assault, Wilton
thought, a daunting smile curving his lips.

Diana, unaware of this scrutiny, was praying for the
music to end. Being so close to Carshin, his arm about
her, was intolerable, and she was conscious only of a
frantic wish that he would vanish from her life.

"Have you forgotten all the plans we made for our
life together?" Carshin said abruptly. Before she could
answer, he hurried on. "We were to have one of the
most elegant houses in London, and fill it with the haut
ton. You would have all the dresses and jewels and
carriages you pleased, and I can assure you that you
would be a great hit—a reigning toast. I have a wide
acquaintance, and I know just where we should find
the best house and whom to invite. It would be
splendid." By this time he was entranced by his own
vision. "How lovely you would be, clothed in the
height of fashion, and rubies—no, emeralds. We would
go to Brighton in the summer. The Prince would
receive us, without doubt. You would be presented at
court, of course. I could guide you as to just how—"

"No," interrupted Diana.

"What?" He looked down, his delightful dream
broken.

"I don't want any of that, particularly not with you."

"You do not want to be a leader of fashion?" Carshin did not really believe this. He could not imagine another ambition than his own dearest wish.

"No."

"But . . . but . . . to live in town."

"I may someday visit London, but I do not need you for that—or for anything."

"On the contrary," he retorted, his temper flaring again. "You will never mingle with the haut ton without me. You will not be accepted in any society if I speak out."

She shrugged. "Then I shall have to do without it." Something in his tone tonight had gradually heartened her. He seemed nearly desperate. And then, with a jubliant flash, she realized Carshin's dilemma. The life he wanted was impossible without her consent. He could ruin her, yes, but by doing so he would also spoil his own prospects. They were at a stalemate. She laughed aloud.

"You find our discussion amusing?" He sneered.

"Yes. For I have just now realized that you can never have what you want."

Meeting her eyes, Carshin saw that she had understood his predicament. The knowledge infuriated him. He felt an almost irresistible impulse to choke capitulation from her lips.

"If you speak," Diana added, "you will lose all chance of your house in town and great position. For you do not come out so well in that story either, and I doubt that any wealthy lady will welcome your addresses when it is known."

"Vixen," he hissed. And Diana laughed again. "You needn't gloat just yet," he went on. "I can still queer things for you. You have hopes of Wilton, do you not? Well, he won't have you. No man will. I shall see to it."

"Even though you have no chance of getting what you want?"

"Yes!"

Diana turned her head away.

"Consider," he urged. "Would you not be happier with me than disgraced and shut away in Yorkshire?" He could see only one answer to this, and his hopes revived.

But Diana shook her head, and, the music ending at last, she walked away abruptly, causing a few stares and titters among the other couples.

Wilton watched it with pleasure. Diana had achieved some sort of victory, he sensed. But the thunderous look on Carshin's face as he strode out of the ballroom told the captain that it was not complete, and his plans remained unchanged.

Diana refused two offers to stand up and sat beside Amanda for the next sets, feeling both elated and distressed. She had at last bested Gerald Carshin in an encounter, and this she had enjoyed immensely. But her situation was really not much better, for he still threatened her heart's desire. Yet Diana could not remain dejected. The music and the crowd, her small triumph, inevitably raised her spirits, and when another waltz struck up and Robert Wilton came up to her, she accepted him with a heart-stopping smile. He responded with one as warm, and they moved onto the floor together.

It was astonishing, thought Diana as she slipped into his arms, how the same steps and posture could be so utterly different. She was intensely aware of Wilton's arm about her waist, and his hand holding hers, and of his shoulder under her fingers, but the sensation was pleasurable and exciting. With Carshin she had wished only to throw off an intrusive touch; now she remembered closer embraces with longing. But even as she moved happily to his direction, another concern surfaced. "I am glad for this opportunity to talk to you," she said.

"Are you? That's good." He smiled down at her again, making her heart beat faster.

"I wanted to ask you about what you said at our last meeting." Though she wanted only to relax in his arms, Diana was determined to speak.

"What I said?" Wilton's tone was warm and loving. He had completed his plan and was feeling at peace with the world. In a very few days, he was certain, his future with Diana would be settled.

"I have the feeling you are plotting something," she blurted, "and it worries me because—"

"Do not allow it to," he responded. "I know what I am about."

"But what is it?"

He simply shook his head.

"Captain Wilton!"

He held her eyes. "Do you not trust me?"

Diana bit her lower lip, trying to find some clue in his face.

"Do you think I would do anything of which you would disapprove?"

"No. Not exactly, but . . ."

"Then do not worry." He smiled, and his blue eyes held such love and admiration that Diana's heart seemed to turn over within her breast. This man deserved the truth, she knew then. She would have to rely on his love to make him understand. "There is something I must tell you," she answered.

But Captain Wilton shook his head. "You needn't."

"Yes. Not . . . not here, but . . ."

He understood that she was ready to reveal whatever Carshin held over her, but it did not matter, he thought. He swung her in a sudden turn, and laughed at her mild startlement. "Let's simply enjoy ourselves tonight," he said. "This is, after all, a ball."

Diana could not resist his smile. Her worry seemed to melt before it. "But, Captain Wilton," she laughed, "I thought you detested balls and all such frivolity."

"Not when I may waltz with *you.*" He pulled her closer. "You have quite changed my opinion."

"But, sir, there is a war going on!" she teased.

Wilton nodded seriously, causing her smile to fade.

"In Belgium," she added, uneasy again over something in his face.

"In Belgium," he agreed, "and other places. But all is well in hand."

"Captain Wilton . . ."

"Someday," he said, "you will call me something other than 'Captain Wilton.' I find I look forward to that very much."

"But—"

"No more, or I will kiss you here and now." He grinned, in high spirits.

Diana could not restrain a nervous look around the ballroom, and Wilton laughed. "For a man who disdains society, you are very bold," she retorted.

"Perhaps I was a bit harsh in my judgment. Some things about society are far from distasteful, I find." He bent his head a little. "The waltz, for example."

For an instant, she almost thought he would kiss her; then he drew back, and Diana let out a sigh that was half relief, half disappointment. Wilton laughed. Diana hesitated, then joined him.

15

THE NEXT DAY DAWNED WARM AND CLEAR, A PERFECT early-summer day, and Diana went through her usual routine with almost her old cheerfulness. At breakfast with the Trents, she teased Amanda gently about her expanding girth; she took a long walk, as she had not done for some time; and over luncheon she joined the discussion of war news, encouraging George to repeat the small store of known facts yet again, his substitute for real information about the course of the campaign.

Amanda, noticing the change, was delighted, and when the two women had a moment alone together and Diana explained the cause of her renewed spirits, she clapped her hands with glee. "You have forced him to a stalemate! He will do nothing now."

"Unless I do," answered Diana, thinking of Wilton.

"Well, yes, but . . . still, it is a step."

She could not help feeling the same herself, and Diana nodded, smiling. Major Trent was heard in the hall, calling his wife.

"Oh, the carriage is ready. I must go. But we will sit down for a real talk after our drive." And with a flutter of gloves, she went out.

Still smiling, Diana sat on the drawing-room sofa and considered what to do with her afternoon. She wished that Captain Wilton might call, but he had said nothing to indicate he would. Indeed, he seemed wrapped up in his own schemes and had not visited them as frequently as before. Diana felt a passing uneasiness, but pushed it down. It was so wonderful to feel herself again; she refused to worry.

The bell rang, and she stood, thinking that her thought had brought Wilton to her. But the maid came in with a card bearing Lord Faring's name. For a moment Diana gazed at it with astonishment. Why should Wilton's brother call on her?

"Shall I show him up, miss?"

"What? Oh, yes, I suppose so."

The girl went out, leaving Diana staring at the card, and soon Lord Faring was standing in the doorway making his bow. It was disconcerting, Diana thought as she greeted him, how little like Captain Wilton he was. The same frame, though without the musculature of a soldier; the same coloring, though washed out by indoor living and excess; the same thin face, though never lit by that entrancing smile.

"You will be surprised by my call," drawled Lord Faring, moving languidly to the chair she offered.

Diana acknowledged this by her silence.

"We are not very well acquainted, but we do have mutual friends. And I come on a mission from one of those. Perhaps two, actually." He leaned back in the armchair, looking quite bored.

Had his brother sent him? wondered Diana. Why?

"I speak chiefly of Gerald Carshin, of course," added the visitor, and she understood. "He has told me of your situation and asked for my help. '

Diana froze. Had Carshin spoken after all? And to Wilton's brother?

"It is unconventional, of course," Lord Faring went on, showing no signs of emotion. "But I do have some connection with the case. Carshin feels that you are rejecting his suit because of my brother, and I am best fitted to speak to you about Robert."

This did not seem like exposure. Diana found her voice. "Really?"

Lord Faring nodded, not seeming to hear the sarcasm. "Had you a father or guardian, I should apply to him, naturally. But Major Trent does not seem to fall in that category, so I am forced to speak directly. Most awkward."

He did not act as if he felt awkward, Diana thought. Indeed, he seemed scarcely interested in the matter. She thought of dismissing him, but she was curious as to what he had to say.

"Carshin's a good fellow, you know. Amusing. Up to every rig and row in town. And he's taken with you. Never seen him like this. Be a good husband."

"I really don't think . . ." began Diana.

"That it's any of my affair. Perhaps not. But if you're on the catch for Robert, perhaps it is, you know."

Diana gasped. "On the—"

"Beg pardon. Wrong way to put it. Not as if you're after a fortune, is it?" He smiled what Diana supposed he imagined was an ingratiating smile. Again she felt the urge to throw him out, but his next words stopped her. "Robert's nothing to boast about, you know. No address, no style, not a particle of town bronze. And his expectations ain't great, mind. He has a little money, but barely enough to set up his household."

Diana stood. She would not listen to this contemptible man criticizing his own brother. "I think you should go."

Lord Faring did not move. "In a moment. Main thing I wanted to say was this. If you're hanging out for a title, you're sadly mistaken."

"A title?" Diana was mystified.

"I shan't stick my spoon in the wall like Richard, not by a long chalk. Catch me near a battlefield! And in time I shall set up my own nursery, so you're fair and far out if you expect Robert to succeed."

"I have no idea what you're talking about," replied Diana. "Who is Richard?"

Lord Faring examined her with narrow eyes, and evidently decided that she was serious. "Brother. Robert is the youngest."

"You have other brothers?"

"Had. Richard was killed in the Peninsula in 1809."

She stared at him, unbelieving. Captain Wilton had never mentioned this to her.

"That's why they tried to keep him home in the beginning and then had him assigned to headquarters staff," added Lord Faring. "And why they won't let him go back."

"It wasn't his knee?"

He made a derisive noise. "There's nothing wrong with Robert's knee. Not now. Wellington merely hopes I'll break my neck and Robert will step into my shoes. Old 'friend' of our family, you know. He's always coddled Robert. My father didn't want another Wilton in the thick of it."

Diana was speechless, trying to take in this information.

"So you see, you shan't be Lady Faring. You may as well take Carshin; he's by far the better man."

"You are contemptible!" Diana blurted, and immediately regretted it.

Lord Faring blinked. "Beg pardon?"

She could not keep silent. "How can you speak of your own brothers that way? And one of them killed!" She turned half away, overcome by the thought of this sorrow that Captain Wilton had not shared with her.

Lord Faring stood, his face even more studiously bland. "My brothers never gave a rap for me. Nor did my father. If one didn't care to risk one's neck at every turn, he lost interest. I owe none of them a farthing." He took a breath. "Good day, Miss Gresham. I hope you will consider what I have said." And with a nod, he went out.

Diana sank down again, bemused. How little she really knew of Robert Wilton, she thought. And yet this new knowledge brought no doubt of her love. Indeed, if anything, it increased it. How dreadful it must have been, to lose his brother in the war. She was extremely glad they had refused to send him back, she thought with a shiver.

Leaning her head on the sofa back and gazing at the ceiling, Diana thought of Wilton with a fond smile. He was so thoroughly admirable, such a stark contrast to Gerald Carshin. Her choice this time was wise.

This brought back her problem, and made her realize that Carshin must be feeling quite desperate to have sent Lord Faring to talk to her. Did he really expect to change her mind? It seemed he did, though she could not imagine why. But if he was uneasy, perhaps there was a chance of beating him after all.

Diana sat up and stretched her arms over her head, more optimistic than she had been in weeks. She would find a way!

Suddenly there was a great crash below as the front door was flung back on its hinges. Booted feet hammered on the stairs, and Captain Wilton ran into the room, closely followed by George Trent. The captain wore his uniform. "Diana, he's done it!" cried Wilton. "He's actually done it!"

"Wilton met us on the road with the news," added George. "It's only just come. I must get to town and find Simmons. Amanda's coming. See to her, Diana." And he ran out again.

"Who's done what?" asked Diana, bewildered. "Is Amanda all right?"

"Splendid!" Without warning, the captain pulled her close and swung her round and round until she was dizzy. "Everything is splendid!"

"Stop, stop! What do you mean? Why are you wearing your uniform?" Was he going to Belgium after all? Diana wondered, a sudden coldness gripping her heart.

Wilton stopped spinning, and looked a bit sheepish. "I couldn't resist putting it on. Foolish, I know."

"But what has—?"

"Wellington's done it! He's beaten Boney for good and all. There was a great battle near Brussels, I think on the eighteenth. The news is sketchy yet. But he has definitely beaten him."

"Oh, Robert!" She flung her arms around his neck and hugged him.

He responded enthusiastically, then laughed. "I said you should call me 'Robert' someday soon, but I didn't know it would take an end to the war."

Diana drew back and smiled up at him. "It is really true?"

"You think it a ruse to get you in my arms? Trent my accomplice?"

"Idiot!"

"It is really true." He kissed her.

"Is it not wonderful news?" said Amanda from the doorway, and the lovers moved apart, startled. "Oh, do not mind me." But they were self-conscious, and Amanda laughed. "We must have a celebration tonight," she added. "With champagne and . . . oh, everything. You will stay, won't you, Captain Wilton?"

"Indeed I shall." He smiled at Diana again.

It was the happiest evening Diana could remember. The men went first to the Pump Room, where all the former soldiers had gathered. Diana and Amanda gave orders for a sumptuous dinner and then retired to change into properly festive gowns. When they met again in the drawing room, George too had donned his uniform, and though they teased him and Wilton, both women found this impulse endearing.

They ate sturgeon and roast beef and ices from the confectioner's, and toasted Wellington and an endless list of his officers in pale champagne. By the end of the meal all four were elevated by the wine, Diana and Amanda, who were not used to it, more so than the men. Indeed, in the drawing room afterward, Amanda insisted upon standing on a footstool and singing George's regimental anthem in a very loud voice. George laughed, but went to lift her down and, still carrying her, said, "Amanda had best go to bed. She must take care of herself. I will say good night."

"I too," said Captain Wilton. George nodded and went out, Amanda waving over his shoulder.

But Wilton did not go at once. He stood looking at Diana and smiling. He was far from befuddled by the champagne; it had only lent a golden sheen to everything around him, most particularly this woman he loved. She seemed the most beautiful he had ever beheld.

Diana was exhilarated by the unaccustomed indulgence. She laughed and took a step toward him.

He gathered her into his arms, and they kissed, long

and passionately. Diana gave herself up wholly to it, every part of her responding to his touch. And when at last they drew a little apart, she said, "It seems as if everything were all right now, doesn't it?"

He nodded, and kissed her lightly again. But her words had reminded him that one task remained. "I must go," he replied softly.

"Must you?" Lifting her hand from his shoulder, she very lightly touched his cheek.

"Yes. But I will call tomorrow with news."

"I suppose there will be more details from Belgium in the newspapers."

"No doubt."

She had a puzzling sense that war news was not what he had meant, but it was lost in regret as he took his leave.

"Tomorrow," repeated the captain.

"Yes. Will you come to dinner again? George and Amanda would be glad, I'm sure."

He hesitated. He had thought to come early. But the advantages of a whole evening together occurred to him, and he nodded.

"Till then." Diana looked wistful.

He bent and kissed her lightly again, then stepped back. With a final smile and a small salute, he went out.

Alone, Diana held her arms out at her sides and whirled, making the skirt of her evening dress bell out. But she found that her balance was imperfect, and after tripping and sinking down on the sofa to avoid falling, she giggled at her own foolishness and went slowly upstairs to bed. It was not until she was beneath the covers that she remembered that she had not asked Wilton about his brother.

*   *   *

The captain strode jauntily down the street, hands in the pockets of his uniform breeches, buoyant and elated. Diana, the news of victory, and the champagne all combined to make him feel that this was one of the best moments of his life. And he realized then that it was also the moment to act. The hour was not so very late, and all of Bath was celebrating. He could find his adversary without trouble. His smile fading to determination, Wilton turned toward the center of the town.

He knew the inn where Gerald Carshin was staying, one of the less expensive near the river, but he did not expect to discover him there so early. He went instead to the hotel where Faring had put up. His brother's group was there, drinking champagne and brandy and toasting Wellington and his army along with the crowd. Captain Wilton settled himself in a corner, waving aside the offer of a glass from revelers who noticed his uniform. He did not intend to draw attention to his mission by dragging Carshin from among his friends. He would wait and go out with him.

It was a long vigil. Lord Faring's set rarely ended a carouse before the early hours of the morning, and this occasion had the novelty of purpose. With an actual event to commemorate, they went on and on, ordering fresh bottles until the waiters grew surly.

At last, however, with dawn only a few hours away, they broke up, Boynton and Lord Faring heading for their rooms in the hotel and the others scattering to various other lodgings. Wilton rose and followed Gerald Carshin. The hours of waiting had dissipated the effects of the champagne, and anticipation had kept the captain alert. He now felt as he most often did just before going into battle: intent and aware of everything around him.

Carshin was thinking only of his bed. He was certain

that Faring had put his case persuasively to Diana, and tonight's indulgences had driven his worries from his mind. He was not befuddled—countless nights of far greater dissipation in London had given him a very hard head indeed—but he was unprepared for anything more taxing than removing his clothes and sleep. When Wilton spoke his name just outside the inn door, he started violently and whirled as if to face footpads. "Wha . . . who is it?"

"Robert Wilton."

He peered at him in the dim street. "Wilton? What are you doing here?"

"I want to talk to you."

"Now? It's after three."

"Now. Shall we go in?"

Automatically Carshin rang, and after a few minutes the landlord came to let them in, growling about the lateness of the hour. Carshin waved him off, and he returned gratefully to bed.

"A private parlor?" suggested Wilton.

By now both curious and intrigued, Carshin indicated a door, and they went inside, Wilton shutting it behind them. The last embers of a fire remained, yielding enough light for Carshin to see to kindle a lamp. Then he turned and surveyed his visitor. "Put on your uniform for the great day, did you?" He sneered. "Touching." Now that he had had time to gather his wits, Carshin found this development very interesting. Wilton's visit must have to do with Diana. Could Lord Faring have caused such an immediate effect? Was this her response?

Carshin moved to the fireplace and stirred the coals, adding fresh wood to create a blaze. He felt only interest and anticipation, for in his eyes Wilton was a poor opponent. He had encountered him occasionally in town when the captain had been persuaded by his mother to join in the festivities of the season, and Carshin judged his address and manner hopeless. He had also absorbed Lord Faring's contempt for his socially inept younger brother, which did not acknowledge, of course, his accomplishments in other fields. Altogether, Carshin felt an amused superiority as he sat in an armchair before the hearth and crossed one leg over the other. "Did you want something?" he asked.

Wilton remained standing. "Yes. I came to speak to you about Miss Diana Gresham."

How ham-handedly direct he was, thought Carshin, a supercilious smile spreading across his face. This would be almost too easy. "Indeed?"

"It is clear to me that you have been annoying her. This must cease."

For a moment what he saw as Wilton's effrontery kept Carshin silent and staring. The idiot actually spoke as if he had some advantage. He was apparently too stupid to realize that he was helpless in Carshin's practiced hands. He must be even less knowing than Faring had said. Carshin hardly knew how to reply to such clumsiness. "Does Diana say that I have annoyed her?" he replied finally, using Diana's first name as a calculated barb.

It struck home, but Wilton ignored it. "She has no need to do so; it is obvious."

"I see. And did Diana send you here to me?"

"No."

"Then what, my dear captain, is your interest in this matter? Though I do not admit that I have 'annoyed' anyone."

"Miss Gresham and I am going to be married, and I forbid you to speak to her or of her ever again."

Carshin laughed. "Such high flights. You should go on the stage, Captain Wilton. Do you claim that Diana has accepted you?" He reached inside his coat and drew out a silver snuffbox, flicking it open with his thumb.

"She has," answered Wilton. And he felt this to be no more than the truth, if perhaps stretched a little.

Carshin was still for a moment; then he proceeded to take the snuff, making of it a prolonged and careful ritual. Finally, when he had brushed the crumbs from his waistcoat with a handkerchief and replaced the box, he said, "Impossible. Diana will marry me, or no one."

"You!" Wilton found the idea revolting.

The other merely nodded. "She is mine, Wilton. You may as well go back to your marching and maneuvers. You have no chance here."

"On the contrary, it is you who will go."

Carshin was becoming bored. He was tired and ready for sleep, and this bumpkin was too dull to provide the least amusement. Toying with him was fruitless; he did not even understand the process. Carshin must be as blunt as he. He had decided at an early moment to tell Captain Wilton the whole story—it would be so amusing to see his reaction, and would remove a rival from the field once and for all—but he had thought to prolong the enjoyment, dropping hints and letting him work it out for himself. This was clearly impossible. The man could not work out a betting sheet. "Diana belongs to me," he replied. "She eloped with me at seventeen, and spent the night in my arms before returning to her home." Seeing the shock in Wilton's face, he maliciously added, "What a beauty she is, eh? You should see that hair all down over naked shoulders and—"

"You lie!" The thought of this worm touching Diana turned Captain Wilton's stomach. He had not devoted much thought to the reasons behind her predicament, once he had satisfied himself that it existed. But whatever thoughts he had had, none had approached this.

Enjoying his horror, Carshin shook his head. "Ask her yourself. She cannot deny it. She has no more forgotten that night than I."

"Why are you not married now, then?" Wilton forced out.

"Ah." For the first time a bit uneasy, Carshin looked away. "A small contretemps concerning the lady's fortune."

"You ruined her, then abandoned her over money?" Wilton ruthlessly suppressed his shock and concentrated on his feelings about this man. Fury and contempt battled in his breast.

"An unfortunate necessity. But I am prepared to make amends now. We shall be wed as soon as possible."

"No." Of the few certainties left Wilton, this one was most clear. Diana did not wish to marry this blackguard.

"My dear sir, there is nothing you can do—"

"She doesn't like you. A child can see that. You will leave her alone."

Carshin began to get angry. "Her preferences are not at issue. She will have me or the world will know of our elopement." He smiled triumphantly.

This was it, then, thought Captain Wilton. This was the threat that had changed Diana from a carefree, laughing girl to a melancholy recluse. Gazing at Carshin's fat complacent face, the captain almost laughed. Did the man really believe it was so easy?

He shook his head. "If you ever come near Diana Gresham again," he said, "or so much as mention her name, I will kill you."

Carshin pulled back in his chair, aghast.

"I will discover some pretext," continued Wilton, "and I will challenge you. I am rather good with sword and pistol, and I shan't stop until you are dead. You will not escape me. I will follow you wherever you go and call you out."

"Are you mad? Dueling is forbidden. You would have to flee the country. You—"

"I have lived abroad for many years. I rather like it. And I should have the satisfaction of knowing that you were dead."

Carshin stood and backed around the chair. Why had he not noticed the terrifying implacability of Wilton's expression before? he wondered. "I could speak before you reached me," he said in a quavering voice. "The girl would be ruined in any case."

Wilton smiled without humor. "True. But you would be dead. I cannot agree with those who argue the former is the worse fate."

"I . . . This is merely a bluff. You would not—"

"I assure you I would."

Meeting Wilton's blue eyes, hard as cold steel, Carshin was convinced. The man must be mad. His only wish now was to escape. "Very well," he said, his dreams of riches once more falling about his ears. "I shan't speak of it. But I can hardly promise never to come near the chit again. In Bath, one often encounters—"

"Yes. That is why I suggest you leave this morning, as soon as may be."

"But that is scarcely three hours . . ."

Captain Wilton shrugged and turned away, his

purpose accomplished. He now wanted only to obliterate all memory of this man from his mind. His personality sickened him.

"How am I to explain to my friends, your brother?"

If he had thought by this to gain some measure of sympathy, he was sadly mistaken. "I don't care a damn what you say," replied Wilton, moving toward the door. "Or what you do, so long as I need never see you again." And with a sharp jerk of the oak door, he was gone.

Carshin heard the outer door of the inn bang, and sank into the armchair, running shaking hands through his hair. Never in his life had he faced the threat of physical violence, and he decided he was quite unsuited for it. He felt dizzy and sick. "Barbarian," he muttered, then wiped his mouth with the back of his hand. But he could think of no way to evade the captain's threat. He was convinced the man would carry out his promise.

And so this lout would get the heiress, he thought, grinding his teeth, and he was back where he had started. They could come to London and gloat over his failure, and he could do nothing. His revelation had not seemed to discourage Wilton, though Carshin was not surprised, for he would not have thrown away a fortune for such a reason. But at least he had given the man something to think of when he held his bride in his arms. The picture he had painted had shaken Wilton; he had seen that. And it would rise again and again. That was something.

Suddenly Carshin had another thought, one which made him smile despite his disappointment. Diana had been most upset at the idea that Wilton might be told the truth. She should not be allowed to escape scot-free.

His smile widening, Carshin moved to the writing desk in the corner of the room, carrying the lamp with him. He had promised never to see Diana again, he thought as he found paper and pen; he had not sworn he would not write. That pair should have much to talk over when next they met. Laughing a little, he wrote, "My dear Miss Gresham," at the top of the sheet.

16

DIANA BREAKFASTED ALONE THE NEXT MORNING, AS was now usual. Thus it was not until she finished eating and went to inquire if Amanda wanted anything from town, where Diana intended to walk, that she received Carshin's missive. The letters were always taken to Amanda with her breakfast tray. Diana's correspondence was limited to the bankers in Yorkshire and an occasional bill.

She was surprised, therefore, when Amanda held out the envelope, saying, "There is a letter for you. I would have had it taken downstairs, but I knew you would be up."

"For me?" She shook it and looked at the direction. The handwriting was unfamiliar. "What can it be?"

"I know how to find out," answered Amanda.

Smiling, Diana tore it open. But her pleased expression soon faded to apprehension as she glanced at the signature, then horror as she read, "This is to inform you that I had an extremely interesting conversation with Captain Robert Wilton last night. I am leaving Bath, and you may think you have won. But the captain now knows all about you, and you may find his feelings quite altered."

"Diana, what is it?" exclaimed Amanda, sitting bolt upright in her bed. "You have gone white as chalk. Is it bad news?"

Wordlessly Diana handed her the note. Amanda read it quickly, then let the paper drop on the counterpane. "Oh, no."

Diana felt as if she had been encased in ice. Even her heart seemed to have ceased beating.

Her friend searched for comforting words, and found none. She picked up the letter again. "He says he is leaving Bath, and that you have won. Do you suppose he means to let you be? He must. He says nothing about meeting you again. But why? I wonder what Robert Wilton—?"

"What does it matter?" blurted Diana. "He has told the story. I suppose everyone in Bath is talking of it by now. And sneering behind their hands."

"He says only that he has told Robert. You do not think Captain Wilton would repeat . . ."

"Of course not. But Carshin would not stop there. Why should he?" Diana paused to swallow a lump in her throat. "Besides, if Captain Wilton knows . . ."

The two women were silent for a long moment, contemplating this disaster. Amanda longed to say that it would make no difference, but she did not believe it. No man could help but be affected by such a revelation, she thought, and the ones she knew best—George, her father—would have been outraged and repelled. She imagined herself in such a situation, before her marriage. George would have rushed from her directly to the battlefield, she thought, and played the reckless care-for-nobody hero. She would probably have pined away at home, thinking of him. There would have been no match. Tears filled her eyes at the vision; then she shook her head at her own idiocy. This was no way to aid Diana. "You can't be certain the story is spread," she offered. "Something has happened." She concentrated. "Indeed, I think Captain Wilton has driven Carshin off. Why else would he go so suddenly?"

Thinking over the events of the last few days, Diana was forced to agree. "He has been planning something."

"Robert?"

She nodded.

"There! He has saved you. Just like a knight in a fairy tale." Diana looked at her, and she faltered. "That is . . ."

"And Carshin has retaliated by telling him the truth. And so I *am* ruined, though I may continue to live in society as long as I please."

"Diana . . ."

"I care more for his good opinion than any other's! Indeed, had I that, I should not mind what . . ." She choked, unable to go on. Amanda got out of bed and came to put her arm around her shoulders. "Oh, Amanda, what am I to do?"

"You . . . you can talk with him. Perhaps . . ." But she could not finish.

Diana imagined facing Wilton under these new circumstances. The thought made her wince. If his eyes now held contempt and revulsion instead of love—and how could it be otherwise once she had been linked with a man such as Carshin—she would not be able to bear it. And yet a small flame of hope also flickered. Amanda had understood her plight. Might he not as well? Tonight, when he came to dinner, she could judge the chances.

But at that moment there was a knock at the door and one of the maids came in. "A note, ma'am," she said, holding out a sealed missive. "It is for you and Miss Diana, the man said."

"Man?" said Diana, more sharply than she meant.

The maid gazed at her. "The man what delivered it. He didn't wait."

"Thank you, Annie," said Amanda, and she unfolded the sheet as the girl went out. A silence followed.

"What is it?" asked Diana apprehensively.

Amanda looked up, distressed.

"Amanda. What?"

"It . . . it is from Robert. He begs us to excuse him from dinner tonight as . . . as he has pressing business. He says he will call soon."

Diana did not move. She felt that if she stirred or spoke she would shatter in a thousand pieces on the carpet. She had hoped, she realized. She had not really given up till now.

"Perhaps he does have business," stammered Amanda. "His brother, or . . ."

Carefully Diana shook her head. Then she turned and moved slowly toward the door.

"Where are you going?"

"To my room." Her voice sounded alien in her own ears.

"Are you all right?" As soon as she asked it, Amanda knew the question was ridiculous.

"No."

"What can I do? Will you not stay here? I . . ."

"I will be better alone for a while, Amanda. But thank you." Diana went out, closing the door very quietly behind her. Amanda gazed at it with tears in her eyes, Captain Wilton's note still clutched in her hand.

Robert Wilton would have been astonished and horrified had he witnessed this exchange. But having no knowledge of Carshin's letter, he sat in his lodgings secure in the thought that he had ample time to adjust.

For Carshin's story had indeed shaken him. There could be no denying that. As the Londoner had hoped, the picture he had painted—of Diana in his embrace— haunted Wilton, making him at once furious and sick. Like most men of his class and generation, Robert Wilton had been taught to value innocence in a woman above many other qualities. He had, he saw now, a certain vision of his wife, though he had not been conscious of forming it. Diana had matched all his desires, until this revelation.

Wilton understood far more than Carshin had said. He had no doubt that the blackguard had deceived and misused a naive girl. Even knowing little of Diana's history, he was certain that none of it was her fault. A man such as Carshin was heedless of propriety. Diana had done nothing. But even as he assured himself of this, the vision rose again. He could see it damnably clearly: her golden hair streaming down, her innocent acceptance of Carshin's lying endearments.

With a wordless exclamation, Wilton leapt up and hurled his shaving mug into the grate, where it shattered against the bars. He could not bear it! How could he ever look at Diana again without seeing that picture?

Catching up his riding crop, he strode from the room and down to the stables. If he stayed inside a moment longer, he thought, he would begin to beat on the walls with his fists. A long hard ride was the thing. If he could settle nothing in his mind, at least he would be tired out.

The conventional course of action in his situation— breaking off with Diana while keeping forever silent as to the reason—satisfied him no more than its alternative. He loved her, or had loved her, dearly. He could name her sterling qualities and enumerate her beauties. Never to see her again—the thought made him clench his teeth.

Mounting up, he headed away from the town, pushing his horse hard. The motion eased the turmoil of his brain a little, and he attempted an objective analysis. Nothing had changed in the Diana he loved, he told himself. The incident with Carshin had occurred years ago, and no doubt she had regretted it bitterly. The way she treated Carshin showed her dislike for the man and the memory. She was not even the same person, really, who had been taken in by him.

Yet his anger remained; he could not seem to ease it. Wilton wished for a confidant. If only there were someone he could turn to for advice. If his father were alive . . . But no. He could not share this story and expose Diana to the chance of ruin. And his father's counsel would have been harsh, he suspected.

Spurring his horse, he galloped down a green lane, oblivious of the lush summer vegetation and the scent of roses. It almost seemed as if he could outrun his dilemma, if he went fast enough.

But when he at last pulled his mount to a shivering, foaming halt, his problem was as pressing as ever, and he was no closer to deciding what to do. He walked the animal for a while, and then rode on as the morning turned to afternoon, still wrestling with his desires and prejudices.

At three, Diana came downstairs wearing a bonnet and shawl; she found Amanda alone in the drawing room. The latter rose at once. "Diana, how are you? You missed luncheon. Do you want something?"

"No." Diana hesitated, looking at her. "I'm leaving, Amanda. I'm going home."

"What?"

"I know it is a cowardly thing to do, but I cannot bear to stay. My house is still there. I can hire one or two servants. I will be quite—"

"But you can't go without seeing Robert! Diana, you *must* talk with him. You do not know how he feels. Perhaps—"

"He has let me know. Do you not see that, Amanda? His message today was designed to tell me in a way that hurt less than meeting. It was, I suppose, kind." Tears threatened, and she turned her face away briefly.

Amanda tried to think of objections, but her friend's reasoning seemed depressingly plausible. "You cannot be sure," she answered weakly.

Diana gazed at her. "I am sure."

"But . . . but . . . you needn't return to Yorkshire, to that cold bleak house." She shivered slightly. "No one else knows your story, and I do not think they will. I feel it, somehow. So you can stay with us. We could go to London if you do not like to remain in Bath. Or, since it is so late, Brighton or . . ."

"No," replied Diana softly.

"You would forget him after a time, with the diversion of society."

"Would you have forgotten George so?"

Amanda was silent, looking unhappy.

"Truly I care nothing for society. It has not matched my expectations. I shall be better off alone."

"You won't! How can you say so? I can't bear to think of you living solitary in that house. You have been so much happier since you left it and came to us."

Diana could not dispute this. She did not try. She knew she was reacting in her old pattern, and perhaps wrongheadedly. To hide from the consequences of her actions might be unwise, but she did not feel able to face the alternative. She had always chosen to avoid censure and contention rather than endure the unhappiness they engendered.

"But I will miss you so!" wailed Amanda, giving up reasoned argument. "I thought you would be with me for weeks yet. Months, perhaps. You cannot go."

This was difficult to take. Diana knew she had been a great help to her friend in her current delicate state of health. And their companionship had warmed them both. But Amanda had her family, and she would before long be engrossed by an addition to it. "I'm sorry, Amanda. George will be here."

"Yes, but . . ." She pressed her lips together, and tears spilled over her lashes.

"I am sorry!" cried Diana. "But I cannot help it, I swear. I could not go on as usual after this. I would be of no use to you."

"Perhaps *I* could be useful to *you.*"

"Oh, Amanda." She stepped forward and took both her hands. "You are truly my dearest friend, and if you will sometimes come to visit me at home, I will be grateful. But even you cannot make up for what I have lost."

Amanda held her hands as a lifeline. "You are not allowing enough time!"

Diana gave one last squeeze, shook her head, and moved away. "I am taking Fanny. She has no objection to returning to Yorkshire. I must go and arrange for a post chaise."

"George will be home in a moment. Let him go."

"It isn't necessary."

"Let me do *something!*"

"Amanda, I can't bear sitting still—and thinking. I beg your pardon, but I will go myself. I will say goodbye before setting out." She turned away.

"You can come back anytime you like," blurted Amanda. "Perhaps a stay at home will help, and then you can return to us."

Diana hesitated, hating to disappoint her, though she was certain she would not return. "Perhaps," she replied finally, and went out.

All the arrangements were complete within two hours. The post chaise waited outside the front door of the Trents' lodgings as Diana's things were brought down and loaded. The two women stood together in the drawing room, Amanda watching her friend's face and Diana gazing sadly at the floor. George, who had come home in the meantime, alternated between supervising the servants and joining his wife and guest. "Are you certain you will not wait until morning?" he said for the fourth time when he had seen the last valise carried down. "You have scarcely three hours until dark, and there is no moon."

"I want to get started," answered Diana.

The major shook his head. He was utterly mystified by this sudden start, but clear signals from his wife had kept him more or less silent. "Well, the baggage is loaded."

"Thank you." Diana stepped closer and offered her hand. "I must also thank you for all your kindness to me. You have been the best of hosts, and a good friend."

He clasped her hand a bit awkwardly, seeming even more puzzled. "Why go, then?" he could not restrain himself from saying. It was obvious to George that this parting grieved Amanda, and he would prevent it if he could. "If you hadn't been happy with us, or if there had been a quarrel . . ." He paused, fishing.

"How could there be?" Diana assured him warmly.

He looked from his now tearful wife to Diana, whose

smile was patently forced. "I don't understand any of this."

"I'm sorry. I must go," was Diana's only reply. She did not think she could bear further good-byes. "Fanny is waiting for me in the carriage."

"Oh, Diana!" Amanda ran forward and flung her arms about her friend. "I shall miss you so." She was crying openly.

"And I you."

They clung together briefly; then Diana gently disentangled herself, tears showing on her cheeks as well. "You will visit me."

"Of course."

With an attempt at a smile, and a nod to George, she hurried from the room. Amanda ran to the stairs to watch her go out, and in a few moments they heard the chaise pulling away. "For God's sake, what is going on?" said the major.

His wife shook her head and walked into his arms to be comforted.

He enfolded her. "You're not going to explain, are you?" Silence answered him, and he sighed. "Well, it is a great pity. You were so pleased to have her here." This, not unnaturally, caused Amanda to cry again, and Major Trent cursed his clumsiness and devoted himself to restoring her spirits.

The Trents' dinner that evening was not festive, and when George suggested that they go to a concert, Amanda merely shook her head. The room seemed echoing and overlarge, and the rattle of cutlery intrusive, without Diana's additions to the conversation.

Afterward, they sat in the drawing room, and

George exerted himself mightily to be amusing. But Amanda would not be jollied. Finally, in the midst of an anecdote the major thought uproarious, she said, "The world is really so unfair, George."

"Eh?"

"Nothing happens as it should, and the nicest people are made to suffer for the actions of bad ones."

"Who do you mean?" he responded, puzzled.

"Um?" She looked up as if surprised. "Oh, nothing. Go on with your story. It is very funny."

The major eyed her. "Well, Rollins had bought the chicken, but he had nowhere to cook it. Sergeant Hooker had a fine pot, but nothing to put in it. Yet they were so much at odds that . . ." He paused, aware that Amanda had ceased listening. "That Rollins deserted to the French rather than cook his bird in Hooker's pot," he suggested. Amanda merely nodded. "And so, of course, Hooker led his troop in an assault on the enemy position and recaptured the chicken. He carried it back across the lines in triumph. It made the most frightful row, squawking and flapping its wings. He held its feet and waved it about like a banner."

"Um," said Amanda again.

"And so Wellington gave him a medal and put him in charge of foraging for the entire army. Amanda, what is the matter?"

She started. "What?"

"I have been talking the veriest nonsense for five minutes, and you have not heard a word."

"Yes, I have. It was about . . ."

The major took her hand. "Won't you tell me what's wrong?"

She hung her head. "I can't, George. It is not my secret."

"Secret?" He raised his blond brows.

They were interrupted by the sound of the bell and, just after, footsteps on the stairs. In the next instant, Captain Wilton appeared. "I told the servant you would see me," he said. "I am sorry to call so late, but I must speak to Miss Gresham. It is very important."

Amanda leapt to her feet. "Oh, no!" She put both hands to her lips.

Wilton stared at her, and George looked from one to the other. "Diana left for Yorkshire four hours ago," he said finally.

"Left . . . ?" The captain seemed stunned.

But the major had been diverted. "Amanda, are you all right? You look ill." He went to her and put an arm around her waist. "Come and sit down. You are pale."

"I'm all right."

"Don't be ridiculous. You must take care." He led her back to the sofa and seated her. "Wilton, perhaps—"

"I must talk to Captain Wilton," declared Amanda decisively. "Would you leave us alone, please, George."

"What?"

"It is about Diana, and I must talk with him."

The major appeared torn between hurt and outrage.

"George, please!"

Meeting her pleading eyes, and glancing at Wilton's tense white face, the major gave in. But he was clearly offended at his exclusion.

"I will explain all I can later," offered his wife. With a curt nod, he left the room.

Amanda and Captain Wilton gazed at one another, each trying to gauge the other's knowledge and state. Amanda spoke first. "She did not think you would call again. And so she went home."

"But why should she think that? In my note I said—"

"She judged that a hint you would come no more. Because of Carshin's story."

Wilton stared. "How . . . do you . . . ?"

"She told me the whole. And Carshin wrote to her about you."

"Damn him!" he exploded. "I'll pay him for—"

"Captain Wilton. Why have you come?" Amanda leaned forward and searched his face.

"To . . . to see Miss Gresham."

"And?"

"What do you mean?" He avoided her eyes.

"What did you plan to say to her?"

He turned half away, frowning.

"Please. I am her friend. I know the circumstances. This is not prying."

Wilton turned back and looked at her. Here, unexpectedly, he had perhaps found the confidante he had sought. "I'm . . . not sure. I have spent this whole day thinking—and getting nowhere. It is . . . difficult. But as I was riding home, I realized I had to stop here. I could not stay away. And she has gone!" He looked toward the windows, curtained now against the dark.

"Yes." Amanda still watched him, trying to understand what he felt. "Will you sit down for a moment, please. There is something I should like to tell you."

"I don't know. Perhaps I should . . ."

"It is very important."

Something in her voice brought him to the sofa and made him sit beside her.

There was hope as well as hurt and confusion in his eyes, Amanda saw exultantly. "I don't believe Diana ever spoke to you about her childhood," she began. Wilton shook his head. "Well, I want to do so now."

He looked puzzled but not unreceptive. "Very well."

Amanda took a deep breath, relieved that he meant to listen. She thought for a moment, then began.

She talked for nearly half an hour, without interruption from her visitor. His expression altered with her words, but he did not speak. At last, hoping that she had proved a good advocate, she finished, "It was years ago, and Diana is much changed. I can testify to that."

There was a silence. Amanda bit her lower lip.

"I never imagined it was her fault," said Wilton quietly then. "I do not blame her, precisely. Particularly after what you have told me."

"No one could."

He raised his head and met her eyes. "But it is still very difficult to . . . accept. I don't know if you can understand."

She nodded, sad.

"I feel as if I were being torn in five different directions, and, frankly, I do not know where I shall end up."

"But you intend to talk to Diana," she urged, leaning forward again.

"I did. But if she does not wish to see me . . ."

"She went away because she believed you would not see her, and she could not bear that. You must go after her."

"You think so?" He rubbed his hands over his face. "I am tired and confused. I do not know what is right anymore."

"I'm certain of it," insisted Amanda.

He hesitated, then nodded. "Yes. Yes, you're right. I must see her."

"She meant to stop at a posting house on the road north. She can't have gone too far."

Wilton stood, suddenly determined. "I'll go at once." He glanced at the mantel clock. "It is scarcely ten, and I can travel faster than a laden chaise. I will speak to her before she sets out again tomorrow."

Amanda hadn't quite expected this. "You will ride in the darkness?"

This elicited Wilton's first smile. "I have often done so in Spain. And I shall not even have to worry about bandits here."

She rose to face him. "I wish you the best of luck, then."

"Thank you. I wonder what that may be?" With a wry salute, he turned to go.

"Oh, I wish I could go with you!"

He glanced back over his shoulder. "You have been a good friend. But the rest . . ." He shrugged. "Go to George. He is probably near bursting with curiosity by this time."

Amanda smiled slightly, then bit her lip again as he went out.

17

DIANA HAD TRAVELED THROUGH THE LONG SUMMER evening and twilight and stopped at a small posting house when darkness fell. Sitting in the hired chaise, Fanny in the opposite corner, she had kept her mind carefully blank. It was no good regretting the past, she told herself, and the future held little to anticipate. It was best not to think. Diana watched the passing scenery with wide abstracted eyes, seeing it without registering details. She answered Fanny's occasional remarks, though these grew fewer as they drove and the girl picked up Diana's mood, and she attended to whatever mundane duties the journey entailed. But Diana felt as if she were only half-alive in the carriage; a large part of her was sealed off, perhaps forever, from the joys and pains of the world.

At the inn, they bespoke a room and a late supper, but Diana could not eat, and when she was in bed, sleep did not come. In the quiet darkness it was more difficult to ignore her situation, and as the hours passed, Diana became more and more dejected.

Captain Wilton, riding through the night, his pace necessarily slow, was not much better off. He, too, had given up thinking. It led him round and round the same questions without a glimmer of resolution, and he had taken refuge in action. Fortunately, the way was difficult without light, and keeping to the road and avoiding obstacles required all his faculties. He had a good idea of how far Diana's chaise could have gone in the time elapsed, but it was hard to judge distances without landmarks, and he had often to pause and calculate where he might be. In this way, the night passed rapidly for him, and when the first streaks of dawn appeared on the horizon, he was surprised.

A glance at the rising sun told Robert that he had somehow strayed off the main north road and into a lane, but when he turned his mount and galloped back, concerned in spite of his uncertainties that he would miss Diana, he reached the highway quickly. And another half-hour's ride brought him to the posting house where she was most likely to be. Inquiring, he found he had judged correctly, and he swung down from his horse and went in to order breakfast.

Diana had meant to make a very early start. But her sleeplessness in the first part of the night had given way to exhaustion as morning approached, and she slept heavily until eight, stirring only gradually at Fanny's urging.

"You said to be sure and wake you," the maid said defensively when Diana rose on one elbow and blinked to clear her vision.

"Yes."

"I'm sure I *would* have let you sleep."

"It's all right." Diana felt as if her head were stuffed with cotton batting. "Is there tea?"

"Yes indeed, miss." Fanny indicated a small tray on the side table, then poured out a cup.

Diana drank gratefully, returned the cup, and rubbed her eyes. Feeling a little better, she pushed back the covers. "You needn't help me dress, Fanny. Would you find the postboys and tell them we will be leaving right after breakfast?"

"They're ready now, miss."

"Oh." Feeling slightly flurried, Diana washed and put on her traveling dress. Fanny picked up her night things and toilet articles. In twenty minutes they were walking downstairs together.

"I'll put this in the chaise, miss, shall I?" said the maid, holding up the dressing case.

Diana nodded and went on toward the private parlor where her breakfast would be waiting. But as she opened the door, she heard her name and turned back, to confront Robert Wilton approaching from the taproom.

She gasped, and turned bright red, then ashen, her hand trembling on the doorknob.

For an endless moment they merely stared at one another, each frozen by conflicting impulses. Then Wilton ushered her into the parlor with a light touch on her elbow. He felt her shaking and he wished at the same time both to soothe and flee from it.

Inside, a small table was set for the morning meal. To Diana it seemed ludicrous—this very ordinary scene in such intensely extraordinary circumstances. She almost laughed, but the sound she felt rising in her throat was distinctly hysterical, and she suppressed it.

Wilton understood that it was up to him to begin. Briefly wishing that he knew what he meant to do, he said, "I called at the Trents' to speak to you, and they told me you had gone. I . . . I followed . . . to speak to you."

"Yes?" Diana did not dare hope. For an instant, when she had first seen him, a flame of possibility had blazed, but his tone and behavior had dimmed it again.

"I . . . Shall we sit down? I did not intend to interrupt your breakfast. Please go on."

Did he actually imagine she could sit calmly and eat as they talked? Diana wondered. She shook her head and went to the armchair before the fire. Wilton took its mate opposite. Silence fell again. Captain Wilton searched for words. "I did not imagine Gerald Carshin would write to you," he said at last. "If I had, I would certainly have . . ." He stopped, with no idea how to end this sentence.

Diana gazed down at her clenched fists. "What passed between you and Mr. Carshin?" she found the voice to ask. "How did you . . . ? I don't understand it."

He took up this less-emotion-laden topic eagerly. "I saw that he threatened you. I told him that if he did not give it up, I would kill him."

"What?"

Not quite realizing how strange this sounded to Diana, he recounted the story of their confrontation, keeping his eyes focused on the hearth rug. His military life had made him familiar with violence, and he did not think of his threat as outrageous.

"Do you mean you would really have killed him!" Diana said when he had finished.

Wilton shrugged.

"But . . ." She couldn't find words.

"I knew it was unlikely to be necessary. The man is a coward. Only a coward would prey on women." Absorbed in his story, he met her eyes, and the gaze held as each of them learned things from the other. Diana was genuinely shocked, Wilton realized, and seeing the episode from her perspective, he could not precisely blame her. Diana glimpsed the motives behind the captain's actions; generosity of spirit and, yes, love had guided him, she saw, and his threat had been without malice or enjoyment. She felt a thrill at his gallantry.

"It was the only way to be sure of routing him," blurted Wilton.

"Thank you," said Diana at the same moment.

They paused, embarrassed, then fell into silence again, left with the question of the future. Neither felt able to broach it.

Finally Wilton squared his shoulders and said, "I spoke with Mrs. Trent before I started out. She told me . . . something about your father and the . . . circumstances—"

"I do not place the blame on others," Diana broke in. "Whatever my difficulties, the fault was mine. Others struggle with youth, ignorance, loneliness, harsh rules without doing what I did."

This was brave, thought Wilton. He admired those who did not make excuses. For the first time since they had met in the corridor, he examined her. The morning sun was slanting through the window and lighting her hair to molten bronze. Her face was in shadow, its exquisite contours accentuated. But more than her beauty, he saw her pain, and her determined control of it. He seemed to see in her expression all the years since Carshin had passed from her life. They had molded her almost as the war had him, he thought. And if she had done something to be regretted—as he had, more than once—the mistake had made her an extraordinary woman. Indeed, without it she might have become like the London misses he so disliked, or a dull, shallow countrywoman. He would not have been drawn to her, or come to love her. So, he told himself, though it was still difficult to think of that long-ago incident, he had, amazingly, reason to be grateful for it. The revolutionary nature of this thought made it slow to assimilate, and the silence in the room lengthened.

Diana, concluding that he must be condemning her, clenched her hands even tighter, until her nails dug into her palms and the skin whitened. Why had he come after her? Why could he not have simply let her go and spared them both this scene? Finally, unable to endure it any longer, she rose. "My chaise is waiting. I must go."

He stood to face her. "Diana—"

"I thank you again for helping me. It is . . . good to know that my . . . story will not be common property. And it was . . . kind of you to come and say good-bye. I—"

"I don't say it."

Something in his voice held Diana motionless, her heart pounding chokingly in her throat.

"Why do you think I followed you? I admit I was not sure myself for a while. But some part of me understood and brought me here." He stepped forward.

"What?"

"I love you, Diana. I have told you so before, and my feelings have not changed."

"Even after . . ."

"No. Or perhaps they have changed, in a way. But only because I now understand more about you and why you are so dear to me."

Diana took a shaky breath. She could not quite believe him yet. Everything she had been taught, and her limited experience, told her that he could not still love her. Her harsh father, her distant neighbors, the insinuations of Gerald Carshin, all argued the opposite. Among her acquaintances, only Amanda had taken her part, and she had seemed convinced that Captain Wilton would not. "Are . . . are you saying this out of pity?" she ventured. It seemed an unlikely explanation, but she could think of no other. "You needn't. I shall be quite all right. I can look after myself."

"I know. It is one of the things I admire most about you." He smiled, and Diana waited, puzzled. Was this a withdrawal? "But there is a difference between being capable of managing and being happy, you know. I learned that in Spain." Seeing her expression, he added, "I could get along very well on my own when I first joined my regiment. Indeed, I prided myself on it. Yet that satisfaction soon gave way to routine and isolation, and I feared I was not suited to military life. I nearly sold out before I discovered the value of helping out my fellows and allowing them to help me." He paused then. "I should like to look after you . . . sometimes."

"I don't think . . ."

"Diana." He stepped forward and took both her hands before she could retreat. "This is *not* pity. I love you!"

Still incredulous, she met his eyes and searched them for signs of other feelings. She found none. Slowly, tentatively, she began to believe. It felt as if the sealed part of her were gradually opening, relieving a terrible pressure and constraint.

Watching her gold-flecked eyes shift, Wilton smiled again, more naturally. After a time, Diana returned his smile—shakily, then with growing joy. He laughed and pulled her into his arms, holding her close.

They stood thus for a while, reveling in their new understanding. Then Wilton put a finger under Diana's chin and raised her lips to his. She responded eagerly, all barriers between them gone. The release from the tension each had felt at the beginning of their interview intensified their passion now. Diana clung to him, and his hands moved tenderly over her back as the kiss went on and on.

When at last they drew apart, Diana swayed a little in his embrace. She had endured dreadful anxiety in the last day, and eaten almost nothing. Combined with this new rush of emotion, it was almost too much.

"Are you all right?" he asked.

"Yes."

"Come and sit down." With a sudden movement, he picked her up and carried her to the sofa on the other side of the room. There, he sat down with Diana across his knees. "That's better." And he bent to kiss her again.

They were wholly engrossed for some time, and each was increasingly elated as loving desire erased their previous moods. When they drew apart again, they grinned at one another delightedly.

"When shall we marry?" said Wilton. "I can get a special license in a week. My mother is very thick with a bishop."

Diana laughed. "Why not?"

"Do you mean it? I thought females required a month at least to prepare for such an event."

"Indeed? Well, *I* am not 'females.' " She looked haughty.

"No." His face softened with admiration. "That you are not. But are you serious?"

"If you are, certainly. I have no family and want no grand wedding."

"Family," he groaned. "I suppose my mother will have something to say about this."

Diana stiffened a little. "You think she will disapprove?"

"On the contrary, she will be so excited to have her

first son wed that she will probably invite half the realm." He considered. "You must meet her, Diana."

This reminded her of something. "You have told me so little about your family. Lord Faring said that your brother . . ." She hesitated, fearing to wound him.

"Have you talked with Faring? Yes, Richard was killed." A shadow passed across his face, then cleared. "That was hard, but he died bravely, and we remember him so."

"By why did you never tell me?" It seemed a slight, not to have mentioned this important fact.

He seemed surprised. "The occasion did not arise."

"Indeed? Though we are to share our lives?" Diana was rather offended.

Frowning, he considered. "I see. I hadn't thought of it from your side. I would have told you, of course, eventually. I honestly did not think of it." He paused. "We avoided thinking or talking of such things, you see, in Spain. Comrades were constantly falling in battle. If one began to dwell on it . . ." He shrugged.

"Oh." Diana felt stupid. "I never thought of that. It would be terrible. I'm sorry."

"Why? You could not know." He caressed her deep-gold hair. "We have much to tell one another. I expect it will take years."

This was such a pleasant thought that they merely gazed at each other for a while.

"You will come to London with me, then?" he asked finally.

She nodded. "We must go back to Amanda's first, however. I cannot leave her wondering what has happened."

"Perhaps they will accompany us."

"Oh, I hope so!"

"And afterward, we can go down to Kent. I have a house there, which I hope you will like."

"I shall love it."

He smiled, then kissed her lingeringly again, and Diana gave herself up to the embrace. They were both oblivious of all externals when the door opened and Fanny peeked into the room.

"Miss!" she gasped.

Diana raised her head dreamily, then sat straight. "Oh, Fanny." She took in the girl's bulging eyes and dropped jaw and struggled with a smile. A glance at Robert made this more difficult.

But they rose. "I have come to take Miss Gresham back to the Trents'," said Wilton. "We will be starting soon. You may inform the postboys."

Fanny goggled at Diana, who nodded, then backed out of the parlor. They heard her run down the hallway toward the innyard.

"Oh, dear." Diana was still sensitive at the idea of scandal.

"Forget her," he replied. "We answer only to each other. And you know my opinion."

Diana sighed. "I do not know why I have been so lucky."

"Do you not? Fortunately, you can also rely on my opinion there." And he pulled her close once again.

About the Author

Jane Ashford grew up in the American Midwest. A lifelong love of English literature led her eventually to a doctorate in English and to extensive travel in England. After working as a teacher and an editor, she began to write, drawing on her knowledge of eighteenth- and nineteenth-century history. She now divides her time between New York City and Lakeville, Connecticut.

JOIN THE REGENCY READERS' PANEL

Help us bring you more of the books you like by filling out this survey and mailing it in today.

1. Book title:_____

   Book #:_____

2. Using the scale below how would you rate this book on the following features.

Poor		Not so Good			O.K.			Good		Excel-lent
0	1	2	3	4	5	6	7	8	9	10

                                                                    Rating
Overall opinion of book........................._____
Plot/Story ...._____
Setting/Location ...._____
Writing Style ...._____
Character Development ...._____
Conclusion/Ending ...._____
Scene on Front Cover ...._____

3. On average about how many romance books do you buy for

   yourself each month?_____

4. How would you classify yourself as a reader of Regency romances?
   I am a ( ) light ( ) medium ( ) heavy reader.

5. What is your education?
   ( ) High School (or less)   ( ) 4 yrs. college
   ( ) 2 yrs. college   ( ) Post Graduate

6. Age_____   7. Sex: ( ) Male ( ) Female

Please Print Name_____

Address_____

City_____State_____Zip_____

Phone # (   )_____

Thank you. Please send to New American Library, Research Dept, 1633 Broadway, New York, NY 10019.

More Delightful Regency Romances from SIGNET

(0451)

☐ THE ACCESSIBLE AUNT by Vanessa Gray.   (126777—$2.25)
☐ THE DUKE'S MESSENGER by Vanessa Gray.   (118685—$2.25)*
☐ THE DUTIFUL DAUGHTER by Vanessa Gray.   (090179—$1.75)*
☐ THE WICKED GUARDIAN by Vanessa Gray.   (083903—$1.75)
☐ RED JACK'S DAUGHTER by Edith Layton.   (129148—$2.25)*
☐ THE MYSTERIOUS HEIR by Edith Layton.   (126793—$2.25)
☐ THE DISDAINFUL MARQUIS by Edith Layton.   (124480—$2.25)*
☐ THE DUKE'S WAGER by Edith Layton.   (120671—$2.25)*
☐ A SUITABLE MATCH by Joy Freeman.   (117735—$2.25)*

*Prices slightly higher in Canada

Buy them at your local
bookstore or use coupon
on last page for ordering.

More Regency Romances from SIGNET

(0451)

☐ AN INTIMATE DECEPTION by Catherine Coulter.   (122364—$2.25)*
☐ LORD HARRY'S FOLLY by Catherine Coulter.   (115341—$2.25)
☐ LORD DEVERILL'S HEIR by Catherine Coulter.   (113985—$2.25)
☐ THE REBEL BRIDE by Catherine Coulter.   (117190—$2.25)
☐ THE AUTUMN COUNTESS by Catherine Coulter.   (114450—$2.25)
☐ THE GENEROUS EARL by Catherine Coulter.   (114817—$2.25)
☐ AN HONORABLE OFFER by Catherine Coulter.   (112091—$2.25)*
☐ THE CALICO COUNTESS by Barbara Hazard.   (129164—$2.25)*
☐ A SURFEIT OF SUITORS by Barbara Hazard.   (121317—$2.25)*
☐ THE DISOBEDIENT DAUGHTER by Barbara Hazard.   (115570—$2.25)*
☐ THE NOBLE IMPOSTOR by Mollie Ashton.   (129156—$2.25)*

*Prices slightly higher in Canada

**Buy them at your local
bookstore or use coupon
on next page for ordering.**

SIGNET Regency Romances You'll Enjoy